Sophia James lives in Chelsea Bay, on Auckland, New Zealand's North Shore, with her husband, who is an artist. She has a degree in English and History from Auckland University and believes her love of writing was formed by reading Georgette Heyer in the holidays at her grandmother's house. Sophia enjoys getting feedback at facebook.com/sophiajamesauthor.

Also by Sophia James

Ruined by the Reckless Viscount
A Secret Consequence for the Viscount

The Penniless Lords miniseries

Marriage Made in Money
Marriage Made in Shame
Marriage Made in Rebellion
Marriage Made in Hope

Gentlemen of Honour miniseries

A Night of Secret Surrender
A Proposition for the Comte
The Cinderella Countess

Discover more at millsandboon.co.uk.

THE CINDERELLA COUNTESS

Sophia James

MILLS & BOON

First published in Great Britain 2019
by Mills & Boon, an imprint of HarperCollins*Publishers*
1 London Bridge Street, London, SE1 9GF

Large Print edition 2019

© 2019 Sophia James

ISBN: 978-0-263-08163-3

MIX
Paper from
responsible sources
FSC
www.fsc.org
FSC® C007454

This book is produced from independently certified FSC™ paper to ensure responsible forest management. For more information visit www.harpercollins.co.uk/green.

Printed and bound in Great Britain
by CPI Group (UK) Ltd, Croydon, CR0 4YY

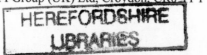

I'd like to thank all my lovely
writing friends from the RWNZ.

Your help and support
have really been appreciated.

Chapter One

London—1815

'There is a man here to see you, Belle, but I warn you he is unlike any man I have ever seen before.'

'Is he disfigured?' Annabelle Smith asked from above her burner where a tincture of peppermint and camphor was coming to a boil nicely, the steam of it rising into the air. 'Or is he just very ill?'

Rosemary Greene laughed. 'Here is his calling card. His waistcoat is of pink shiny satin and he has ornate rings on every one of his fingers. His hair is styled in a way I have never seen the likes of before and there is a carriage outside in the roadway that looks like it comes from a fairy tale. A good one, with a happy ending.'

Annabelle glanced at the card. Lytton Staines, the Earl of Thornton. What could a man like this possibly want with her and why would he come here to her humble abode on the fraying edges of Whitechapel?

'Put him into the front room, Rose, and make certain the dog is not in there with him. I will be there in a moment.'

Rosemary hesitated. 'Do you want me to accompany you?'

'Why should I require that?'

'Our visitor is a young man from society and you are a young woman. Is not a chaperon needed in such circumstances?'

Belle laughed at the worry on her friend's face. 'Undoubtedly if this was society it would be needed, but it is not and he has probably come to purchase medicines. Give me five minutes with this brew and in the meanwhile offer him a cup of tea. If he asks for anything stronger than that, however, do not allow it for we need all the alcohol we have left for the patients.'

Rose nodded. 'He looks rather arrogant and

very rich. Shall I get your aunt to sit with him? I don't think I feel quite up to it myself.'

Belle smiled. 'If we are lucky, the Earl of Thornton might have second thoughts about staying and will depart before I finish this.'

Lytton Staines looked around the room he had been asked to wait in, which was small but very tidy. There was a rug on the floor that appeared as though it had been plaited with old and colourful rags and on the wall before him were a number of badly executed paintings of flowers. He wondered why he had come here himself and not sent a servant in his stead. But even as he thought this he knew the answer. This was his sister's last chance and he did not want another to mess up the possibility of Miss Smith's offering her help.

The woman who had shown him into the front parlour had disappeared, leaving him with an ancient lady and a small hairy dog who had poked its head up from beneath his chair. A sort of mongrel terrier, he determined, his teeth yellowed and his top lip drawn back. Not in a smile, either. He tried to nudge the animal away with his boot in a fashion that wasn't offensive and succeeded only in bringing the hound closer, its eyes fixed upon him.

In a room down a narrow passageway someone was singing. Lytton would have liked to have put his hands to his ears to cancel out the cacophony, but that did not seem quite polite either.

He should not have come. Nothing at all about this place was familiar to him and he felt suddenly out of his depth. A surprising admission, given that in the higher echelons of the *ton* he'd always felt more than adequate.

The cup of tea brought in by a servant a moment before sat on the table beside him, a plume of fragrant steam filling the air.

For a second a smile twitched as he imagined his friends Shay, Aurelian and Edward seeing him here like this. It was the first slight humour he had felt in weeks and he reached for the softness of the emotion with an ache.

Dying became no one, that was for certain, and sickness and all its accompanying messiness was not something he had ever had any dealings with before.

'Thank God,' he muttered under his breath and saw the old lady look up.

He tipped his head and she frowned at him, the glasses she wore falling to the very end of a decent-sized nose and allowing him to see her properly.

Once she must have been a beauty, he thought, before the touch of time had ruined everything. His own thirty-five years suddenly seemed numerous, the down slide to old age horribly close.

With care he reached for the teacup only because it gave him something to do and took a sip.

'Tea was always my mother's favourite drink.' These words came unbidden as Lytton recognised the taste of the same black variety his mother favoured and the frown on the old woman opposite receded.

As he shifted a little to allow the material in his jacket some room, the dog before him suddenly leapt, its brown and white body hurtling through the air to connect with the cup first and his waistcoat second, the hot scald of liquid on his thighs shocking and the sound of thin bone china shattering loud upon the plain timber boards of the floor.

The dog's teeth were fastened on the stranger's clothing. Belle heard the tear of silk and breathed out hard, wondering why Tante Alicia had not reprimanded her pet for such poor behaviour.

'Stanley. Stop that.' She hurried into the front room with horror. 'I am so sorry, sir, but he loves the colour pink and your waistcoat is of the shade he is most attracted to.'

Her hands tried to dislodge the canine's teeth from their sharp hold, but she had no luck at all. If anything, the expensive silk ripped further and she was pulled over almost on top of the Earl of Thornton in the ensuing tangle, her hand coming across the warm wetness at his thighs before he snatched it away.

'Cease.' His voice cut through the chaos and for a moment Belle wondered momentarily if it was to her or to Stanley that he spoke.

Tante Alicia's terrier did just as he was told,

slinking to the door and out of the room with his tail firmly between bowed legs, Alicia herself following.

Annabelle was left in a more compromising position, her balance precarious because of her desperate hope of allowing no more damage to a garment of clothing that looked as if it might be worth more than cost of this entire house put together.

'God, but he has torn it badly,' she said beneath her breath, further words dissolving into French and directed at her departing aunt.

She broke off this tirade when she realised its absolute inappropriateness and regained her feet, crossing to the cabinet by the window and proceeding to extract a pound note from her velvet purse in the drawer.

'I will certainly pay for any damage, sir. I'd hoped Stanley might have been outside in the garden, you see, but unfortunately, he was not.'

'He has a penchant for the colour pink because of a fluffy toy he had as a puppy?' the man asked.

'You speak French?'

'Fluently. I presume that you are Miss Annabelle Smith? The herbalist?'

When she nodded he carried on.

'I am Lord Thornton and I wish to employ your services in regards to my sister. She has been struck down with a wasting sickness and no physician in England has been able to find a cure for her.'

'But you are of the opinion that I might?'

'People talk of you with great respect.'

'People you know?' She could not stop the disbelief betrayed in her words.

'My valet, actually. You were instrumental in allowing his father a few more good years.'

'Yet more often I do not foil the plans of God.'

'You are a religious woman, then?'

'More of a practical one. If you imagine me as the answer to all your…prayers, you may be disappointed.' She faltered.

'I am not a man who puts much stock in prayers, Miss Smith.'

'What do you put stock in, then?'

For a second she thought she saw anger flint before he hid it.

'Brandy. Gaming. Horseflesh. Women.'

There was a wicked glimmer of danger in his gold eyes and Belle stepped back.

Miss Annabelle Smith looked shocked but he was not here to pretend. She had the most astonishing blue eyes Lytton had ever seen and when her fingers had run over his private parts in her haste to remove the dog from the hem of his waistcoat he'd felt an instantaneous connection of red-hot lust.

Hell.

Did the tea have something in it, some herbal aphrodisiac that befuddled his brain and bypassed sense? Because already he wanted her fingers back where they had only briefly rested.

He pushed the money she offered away and stood, his boot crunching the remnants of the teacup into even smaller parts, the roses once etched into the china now disembodied.

He could not imagine what had made him answer her query as to what he put stock in so rudely, but, he suddenly felt just like the dog— Stanley, had she called him?—all his hackles raised and a sense of fate eroding free will.

There was protection in the depravities of his true self and suddenly even his sister's need for Annabelle Smith's magical concoctions was secondary to his own need for escape.

But she was not letting him go so easily, the towel she had in her hand now dabbing again at his thigh.

Was she deranged? What female would think this acceptable? With horror he felt a renewed rising in his cursed appendage and knew that she had seen the betrayal of his body in her instant and fumbling withdrawal. The white towel was stained brown in tea.

'I thought…' She stopped and dimples that he had not known she had suddenly surfaced. 'I am sorry.' With determination she stuck the cloth out for him to take and turned her back. 'You may see to yourself, Lord Earl of Thornton. I should have understood that before.'

His title was wrong. She had no idea how to address a peer of the realm. He rubbed at his thighs with speed and was glad of the lessening hot wetness.

Taking in a breath, he realised how much he

had needed air. She still had not turned around, her shapely bottom outlined beneath the thin day dress she wore. There were patches at a side pocket and the head of some straggly plant stuck out of the top.

She smelt of plants, too, the mist of them all around her. Not an unpleasant smell, but highly unusual. Most ladies of his acquaintance held scents of violets, or roses, or lavender.

'I have finished with the towel, Miss Smith.'

He was amused by her allowance of so much privacy.

'Thank you.' She snatched it back from him and the awkward maiden became once again a direct and determined woman, no air of humour visible.

'I would need to see your sister before I prescribed her anything. Proper medicine does not enjoy guesswork and a wasting sickness encompasses many maladies that are as different from each other as night is to day.'

'Very well. She is here in London for the next week, seeing specialists, so if you would have some time...'

'Pick me up here at nine tomorrow morning. I need to prepare some treatments but…' She hesitated and then carried on. 'I do not come cheap, my lord Earl. Each consultation would be in the vicinity of three pounds.'

Lytton thought she held her breath as she said this, but he could have been wrong. 'Done. I will be here at nine.'

'Good day, then.'

She put her hand out and shook his. He felt small hardened spots on her fingers and wondered what work might have brought those about.

Not the soft pliable hands of a lady. Not the grip of one either. The one ring she wore was small and gold. He felt the excess of his own jewellery with a rising distaste.

A moment later he was in his carriage, leaning his head back against fine brown leather. He needed a stiff drink and quickly.

'White's,' he said to the footman who was closest, glad when the conveyance began to move away from the cloying poverty of Whitechapel and from the contrary, forceful and highly unusual Miss Annabelle Smith.

* * *

His club was busy when he arrived and he strode over to where Aurelian de la Tomber was sitting talking to Edward Tully.

'I thought you were still in Sussex with your beautiful wife, Lian?'

'I was until this morning. I am only up here for the day and will go home first thing tomorrow.'

'Wedded life suits you, then. You were always far more nomadic.'

'The philosophy of one woman and one home is addictive.'

'Then you are a lucky man.'

Lytton saw Edward looking at him strangely and hoped he'd kept the sting out of his reply. It was getting more and more difficult to be kind, he thought, and swallowed the brandy delivered by a passing servant, ordering another in its wake.

He was unsettled and distinctly out of sorts, his visit to the East End of London searing into any contentment he'd had.

'I've just had a meeting with a woman who concocts medicines in the dingy surroundings of Whitechapel. Someone needs to do something about the smell of the place, by the way, for it is more pungent than ever.'

'Was the herbalist hopeful of finding some remedy for your sister?'

Edward looked at him directly, sincerity in his eyes.

'She was.' Lytton said this because to imagine anything else was unthinkable and because right now he needed hope more than honesty.

'Who is she?' Aurelian asked.

'Miss Annabelle Smith. My valet recommended her services.'

'She cured him? Of what?'

'No. She prolonged the life of his father and the family were grateful. I can't quite imagine how he paid the costs, though.'

'The costs of her visits?'

'Three pounds a time feels steep.'

'Had you given her your card before she charged you?'

Lytton nodded. 'And I would have been willing to pay more if she had asked.'

'The mystery of supply and demand, then? How old is she?'

'Not young. She spoke French, too, which was surprising.'

That interested Aurelian. 'Smith is not a French name?'

'Neither is Annabelle. There was an older woman there who did appear to be from France, though. An aunt I think she called her after their dog attacked me.' He loosened the buttons of his jacket to show them the wreckage of his waistcoat.

'A colour like that needs tearing apart.' Edward's voice held humour, but Aurelian's was much more serious.

'I have never heard of this woman or of her French aunt. Perhaps it bears looking into?'

'No.' Lytton said this in a tone that had the others observing him. 'No investigations. She is meeting Lucy tomorrow.'

Edward was trying his hardest to look nonchalant, but he could tell his friend was curious.

'What does she look like?'

'Strong. Certain. Direct. She is nothing like the females of the *ton*. Her dress was at least ten years out of date and she favours scarves to tie her hair back. It is dark and curly and reaches to at least her waist. She was…uncommon.'

'It seems she made quite an impression on you then, Thorn? I saw Susan Castleton a few hours back and she said you were supposed to be meeting her tonight?'

'I am. We are going to the ballet.'

Susan had been his mistress for all of the last four months, but Lytton was becoming tired of her demands. She wanted a lot more than he could give her and despite her obvious beauty he was bored of the easy and constant sex. God, that admission had him sitting up straighter. It was Lucy, he supposed, and the ever-close presence of her sadness and ill health.

He wished life was as easy as it used to be, nothing in his way and everything to live for. One of his fingers threaded through the hole in his waistcoat and just for a second he questioned what ill-thought-out notion had ever convinced him to buy clothing in quite this colour.

It was Susan's doing, he supposed, and her love of fashion. Easier to just give in to her choice of fabric than fight for the more sombre hues. He wondered when that had happened, this surrender of his opinion, and frowned, resolving to do away with both the excessive rings and the colour pink forthwith.

Miss Annabelle Smith was contrary and unusual and more than different. He could never imagine her allowing another to tell her what to wear or what to do. Even with the mantle of poverty curtailing choices she seemed to have found her exact path in life and was revelling in it.

Belle awoke in the dark of night, sweating and struggling for breath. The dreams were back. She swallowed away panic and sat up, flinting the candle at her bedside so that it chased away some of the shadows.

The same people shouting, the same fear, the same numbness that had her standing in the room of a mansion she had never recognised. She thought she hated them, these people, though she was not supposed to. She knew she wanted to run away as fast as her legs could carry her and although she could never quite see them she understood that they looked like her. How she would know this eluded sense, but that certainty had been there ever since she had first had the nightmares when she was very young. Sometimes she even heard them speak her name.

The sound of the night noise from the street calmed her as did the snoring of her aunt in the room next door. At times like this she was thankful for the thin walls of their dwelling, for they gave her a reason to not feel so alone.

The visage of Lytton Staines, the Earl of Thornton, floated into her memory as well, his smile so very different from the clothes he wore.

She remembered the hardness of male flesh beneath the thin beige superfine when her fingers had run along his thighs by mistake. Her face flamed. God, she had never been near a man in quite such a compromising way and she knew he had seen her embarrassed withdrawal.

The incident with the spilled tea this afternoon began to attain gigantic proportions, a mistake she might relive again each time she saw him which would be in only a matter of hours as he was due to collect her in the morning at nine. She needed to go back to sleep. She needed to be at her best in the company of Lord Thornton because otherwise there were things about him that were unsettling.

He was beautiful for a start and a man well used to the exalted title that sat on his shoulders. He was also watchful. She had seen how he'd glanced around her house, assessing her lack of fortune and understanding her more-than-dire straits.

She wondered what he might have thought of her paintings, the flowers she lovingly drew adorning most of one wall in the front room. Drawing was a way for her to relax and she enjoyed the art of constructing a picture.

In her early twenties she had drawn faces, eerie unfamiliar ones which she had thrown away, but now she stuck to plants, using bold thick lines. The memory of those early paintings summoned her dreams and she shook off the thought. She would be thirty-two next week and her small business of providing proper medicines for the sick around Whitechapel was growing. She grimaced at the charge per visit she had asked the Earl to pay, but, if a few consultations with the sister of a man who could patently afford any exorbitant fee allowed many others to collect their needs for nothing, then so be it. Not many could pay even a penny.

He'd looked just so absurdly rich. She wondered where he lived here in London. One of the beautiful squares in the centre of Mayfair, she supposed. Places into which she had seldom ventured.

Would it be to one of those town houses that he would take her in order to tend to his sister? Would his family be in attendance? Alicia had told her the Earl had mentioned a mother who enjoyed tea.

She had not addressed him properly. She had realised this soon after he had left because she had asked Milly, the kitchen maid, if she knew how one was supposed to speak to an earl. The girl had been a maid in the house of a highly born lord a few years before.

My lord Earl was definitely an error. According to Milly she could have used 'my lord' or 'your lordship', or 'Lord Thornton'. Belle had decided when she saw him next she would use the second.

At least that was cleared up and sleep felt a

little nearer. She had prepared all the tinctures, medicines and ointment she would take with her to see Lord Thornton's sister so it was only a case of getting herself ready now.

What could she wear? The question both annoyed and worried her. She should not care about such shallow things, but she did. She wanted suddenly to look nice for the mother who enjoyed tea. That thought made her smile and she lay back down on her bed watching the moon through undrawn curtains.

It had rained yesterday, but tonight it was largely clear.

As she closed her eyes, the last image she saw before sleep was that of the Earl of Thornton observing her with angry shock as she had wiped away the hot tea from his skin-tight pantaloons.

Chapter Two

Miss Smith was sitting on the front doorstep of her Whitechapel house when his carriage pulled up to the corner on the dot of nine. She held a large wicker basket in front of her, covered almost entirely by a dark blue cloth.

The oddness of a woman waiting alone outside her home and completely on time had Lytton waving away the footman as he jumped down to the ground.

Miss Annabelle Smith appeared pleased to see him as she stood, her hand shading her face and the odd shape of her hat sending a shadow down one side of her cheek.

'I thought perhaps you might have decided not to come,' she said, her fingers keeping the cloth on her basket anchored in the growing breeze.

The heightened notice of her as a woman he'd felt yesterday returned this morning and Lytton shoved it away.

'My chaperon will be here in just a moment as Aunt Alicia would not settle until I agreed to have her with me. I hope that is all right with you, your lordship?'

She knew, now, how to address him. He found himself missing the 'my lord Earl'.

'Of course.' The words sounded more distant than he had meant them to be. She looked tired, dark circles under her eyes, and there was a cut on her thumb. He hoped the injury had not come about in the preparation of his sister's medicines.

Pulling the three pounds he had ready from his pocket, he offered them to her.

'If it is too much I quite understand,' she said, but he shook his head.

'I can afford it, Miss Smith, and I am grateful that you would consent to attending my sister at such short notice.'

The same velvet purse he had seen yesterday came out of her pocket, the notes carefully tucked within it.

'It will be useful to buy more supplies for those who cannot pay. There are many such folk here.'

'You have lived in this house for a while?'

'We have, your lordship. It is rented, but it is home.'

'Yet you do not speak with the accent of the East End?'

She looked away, distracted as the same woman he had seen yesterday joined them, busy fingers tying the ribbons on her bonnet.

'This is my friend, Mrs Rosemary Greene.'

'We met briefly yesterday. Ma'am.' He tipped his head and the older woman blushed dark red, but was saved from answering as Annabelle Smith caught at her arm and shepherded her towards the conveyance. When the footman helped each of them up Miss Smith took a deep breath, giving Lytton the impression she did not much wish to get in. He took the seat opposite them as the door closed, listening to the horses being called on.

'Did you ever read the fairy tale *Cendrillon* by Charles Perrault, your lordship?' Her dimples were on display, picked out by the incoming sunshine.

'I did, Miss Smith.'

'Your carriage reminds me of that. Ornate and absurdly comfortable.'

'You read it in French?'

'When I was a child I lived in France for a time with my aunt.'

The traffic at this time of the morning was busy and they were travelling so slowly it seemed as if all of London was on the road.

The silence inside the carriage lengthened, their last exchange throwing up questions. She did not give the impression of one born abroad for her words held only the accent of English privilege and wealth. How could that be?

He hoped like hell that any of his extended family would not converge on his town house this morning, for he wanted to allow Miss Smith some time to talk with his sister by herself. His mother would be present, of course, but she was lost in her own sadness these days and appeared befuddled most of the time. Today such confusion would aid him.

It was as if Lucy's sickness had ripped the

heart out of the Thorntons and trampled any happiness underfoot. It was probably why he had taken up with Susan Castleton to be honest, Lytton thought, her sense of devil-may-care just the attitude he had needed to counter the constant surge of melancholy.

Miss Smith was watching the passing streets with interest, her fingers laced together and still. When they went around a sharp corner, though, as their speed increased he saw her grasp at the seat beneath her, each knuckle white.

'It is perfectly safe. My driver is one of the most skilled in London.'

Blue eyes washed over him and then looked back to the outside vistas.

'People more usually come to see me, your lordship.'

'You don't use hackneys, then?'

'Never.'

This was stated in such a way that left little room for debate and Mrs Greene caught his eye as he frowned, an awkward worry across her face.

Portman Square was now coming into view,

the façade of his town house standing on one corner. He hoped that Annabelle Smith would not be flustered by the wealth of it, for in comparison to her living quarters in Whitechapel it suddenly looked enormous.

As they alighted an expression unlike any he had ever seen briefly crossed her face. Shock, he thought, and pure horror, her pallor white and the pulse at her throat fast. His hand reached out to take her arm as he imagined she might simply faint.

'Are you well, Miss Smith?'

He saw the comprehension of what she had shown him reach her eyes, her shoulders stiffening, but she did not let him go, her fingers grabbing at the material of his jacket.

Then the door opened and his mother stood there, black fury on her face.

'You cannot bring your doxies into this house, Thornton. I shall simply not allow it. Your valet has told me you were in the company of one of your mistresses, Mrs Castleton, last night and now you dare to bring in these two this morning. Your father, bless his soul, would be rolling in his grave and as for your sister...'

She stopped and twisted a large kerchief, dabbing at her nose as she left them, a discomfited silence all around.

'I am sorry. My mother is not herself.'

It was all he could think to say, the fury roiling inside him pressed down. He needed Annabelle Smith to see his sister, that was his overriding thought, and he would deal with his mother's unexpected accusations when he could.

The Earl of Thornton kept mistresses and his mother thought she and Rosemary were fallen woman? The haze of seeing the Thornton town house dispersed under such a ludicrous assassination of her character and if there had not been a patient inside awaiting she would have simply insisted upon being taken home.

This behaviour was so common with the very wealthy, this complete and utter disregard for others, and if the Earl had somehow inveigled her into thinking differently then the more fool she.

It was why Belle had always made it a policy to never do business with the aristocracy, her few very early forays into providing remedies for the wealthy ending in disaster. They either did not pay or they looked down their noses at her. However, she'd had none of the overt hatred shown by the Earl's mother.

Well, here at least she had already been paid, the three-pound fee tucked firmly into her purse.

The Earl looked furious, the muscles in his jaw working up and down and as they entered into the entrance proper he asked them if they might wait for just a moment.

'Yes of course, your lordship.' As Rosemary answered she drew Annabelle over to a set of comfortable-looking armchairs arranged around a table, a vase of pastel-shaded flowers upon it that were made of dyed silk.

Belle sat in a haze, the smell of polish and cleaning product in the air. Everything was as familiar as it was strange and she could not understand this at all. She had seen a house just like this one in her dreams: the winding staircase, the black and white tiles, the numerous doors that led off the entrance hall to elaborately dressed and furnished salons, portraits

of the past arranged solemnly on the walls up
and down the staircase.

'What on earth is wrong with you, Belle? You
look like you have seen a ghost.'

'I think I have.'

'I cannot believe the Earl's mother would
have thought we were doxies.' Rose looked
horrified as she rearranged the red and green
scarf draped about her neck into a more con-
cealing style.

'She has probably never seen one before and
I suppose we dress differently from the people
who live around here.'

Belle hoped the woman would not return to
find them again just as she prayed she could
have asked for her coat and hat and left.

But she'd been paid well for a consultation
and the carriage outside had rumbled on already down the street. Their only avenue of
escape was the Earl. He suddenly came down
the passageway to one side, another servant accompanying him.

'My sister's suite is this way. There is a sitting room just outside if Mrs Greene would feel
comfortable waiting there.'

Rose nodded and so did Belle, this visit becoming more and more exhausting. She did not truly feel up to the task of reassuring a young, sick and aristocratic patient, but had no true way to relay that to the Earl of Thornton without appearing ridiculous. Still, if his awful mother was there with more of her accusations she would turn and go.

As they mounted the staircase the smell of camphor rose from her basket and Annabelle presumed the container in it had fallen over. Removing the fabric, she righted it and jammed it in more tightly against the wad of bandages at its side.

The light was dimmer now and the noises from the street and the house more distant. The scent of sickness was present, too, her nostrils flaring to pick up any undertones of disease. Surprisingly there were none, a fact that had her frowning.

'If you could wait here, Mrs Greene, it would be appreciated. My sister in her present state is not good at receiving strangers and one new face is probably enough for now.'

Seeing Rose settled Belle followed the Earl

through a further anteroom, which opened into a large and beautiful bedchamber, full of the accoutrements of ill health and all the shades half-drawn. There were medicine bottles as well as basins and cloths on a long table. Vases full of flowers decorated every other flat surface.

At the side of the bed a maid sat, but she instantly stood and went from the room, though there had been no gesture from the Earl to ask her to leave.

'Lucy?' The Earl's voice was softer, a tenderness there that had been missing in every other conversation Belle had had with him. 'Miss Smith is come to see you. The herbalist I told you of.'

'I do not want another medical person here, Thorn. I've said that. I just want to be left alone.'

The tone of the voice was strong. A further oddness. If Lady Lucy had been in bed for this many weeks and deathly ill she would have sounded more fragile.

She had burrowed in under the blankets, only the top of her golden head seen. Her fingernails were bitten to the quick, every single one of them, but there was no discolouration of the nail beds.

'Miss Smith is well thought of in her parish of Whitechapel. She seldom visits outside her home area, so in this we are more than fortunate.'

'Where is Mother?'

'I asked her to stay in her room.'

'She is being impossible this morning. I wish she might return to Balmain and leave me here with you. How old is Miss Smith?'

'See for yourself. She is right here.'

The blanket stilled and then a face popped out from the rumpled wool. A gaunt face of wrecked beauty, the hair cut into slivers of ill-fashioned spikes.

Belle hoped she did not look surprised, the first impressions between a patient and a healer important ones.

'You are not too…old.' This came from Lucy.

'I am thirty-two next week. It seems inordinately old to me. But what is the alternative?'

Unexpectedly the young woman smiled. 'This.'

'Perhaps,' Belle said quietly. 'When did you last eat?'

'I am no longer hungry. I have broth sometimes.'

'Could I listen to your pulse?'

'No. I don't like to be touched.'

'Never?' Surprise threaded into her words. 'Who has examined you then?'

'No one. I do not allow it. It can be seen from a distance that my malady is taking the life from me. All sorts of medicines have been tried. And have failed. One doctor did touch me against all my will and bled me twice. Now I just wish to die. It will be easier for everyone.'

Belle heard the Earl draw in a breath and felt a huge sorrow for him.

'Could I sit with you for a moment, Miss Staines? Alone?'

'Without my brother, you mean. Without anyone here. I do not know if...'

But the Earl had already gone, walking like a ghost towards the door, his footsteps quiet.

Belle waited for a moment and closed her eyes. There was so much to be found in silence. The girl's breathing was fast and a little shallow, but there was no underlying disease in her passageways. She moved her feet a lot, indicating a nervous disposition. She could hear the sound of the sheets rustling and Lady Lucy sniffed twice. She was coming down with a cold, perhaps, though her constitution sounded robust.

Opening her eyes, Belle looked at her patient directly, the golden glance of the Earl's sister flecked with a darker yellow.

'Why do you lie, Miss Staines?'

'Pardon?' A shocked breath was drawn in with haste.

'There is no disease in your body. But what is there is something you need to speak of.'

'You cannot know this.' These words were small and sharp.

'Today I shall run camphor across your chest and peppermint under the soles of your feet. If I was you, I should then begin to take an interest in the world. Tomorrow I shall return with different medicines. A week should be enough for you to start getting up again and then we can face the problem that is the true reason why you have taken to your bed.'

'Problem?'

'Think about it. Your family is suffering from the charade you are putting them through and if the physicians they have dispatched to attend to your needs have never delved deeper into the truth of what ails you then that is their poor practice. But it is time now to face up to what has happened to you and live again in any way that you can.'

'Get out.'

Belle stood, her heart hammering. 'I am sorry, but I will not. Only with good sense can you face what must come next because, believe it or not, this is the way of life. A set back and then a triumph. Yours will be spectacular.'

'Are you a witch, Miss Smith? One of the occult?'

'Perhaps.' Her reply came with a fervour. This girl needed to believe in her words or otherwise she would be lost. 'Magic is something that you now require so I want you to unbutton your nightdress and I will find my camphor.'

* * *

Ten minutes later she was downstairs again and the Earl of Thornton had recalled his conveyance.

'I am sorry I cannot accompany you back to Whitechapel, Miss Smith, but I have other business in the city. You said that you'd told my sister that you would be back on the morrow so I shall make sure my conveyance is outside your house again at nine.'

'No. Tomorrow we shall find our own way. But have the maid bring up a plate of chicken broth with a small crust of bread for your sister. Tell her that such sustenance will do her good and I will be asking after how much she has eaten.'

'Very well. Thank you.'

The Earl did not believe that his sister would deign to eat anything. He was disappointed in her short visit, too, Belle could tell, the smell of camphor and peppermint the only tangible evidence of her doctoring. He imagined her a quack and a charlatan and an expensive one at that and would continue to do so unless his sister took her advice.

She tipped her head and turned for the pathway, unsurprised when the door was closed behind them.

Once home she sought out her aunt where she sat in the small alcove off the kitchen.

'I recognised the Earl of Thornton's house, Tante Alicia. I think I knew one just like it.'

Her aunt simply stared at her.

'It was similar to the house in my dreams. The one I told you about.'

'I always said that you were an auld one, Annabelle, a traveller who has been here before in another lifetime.'

'Who are they, Alicia? The people I remember who are dressed like those at the Thornton town house.'

'I have told you again and again that there are no ghosts who stalk you and that I do not know of these people you see.'

'Then who were my parents?'

'I never met them. I took you in when a nun from the convent in the village asked it of me. A sick child from England who was placed in the hands of the lord when a servant brought her there, to the church of Notre-Dame de la Nativité. Maria, the nun, was English herself and spoke with you every day for years until your French was fluent and you could cope. That is all I know. I wish there had been more, but there was not. I'd imagined you would stay with me for only a matter of weeks, but when no one came back to claim you and the months went on...' She stopped, regathering herself. 'By then you were the child I had never had and I prayed to our lord every day that the situation would continue, that I would not have to give you up because that would have broken my heart.'

They had been through all this before so many times. It all made perfect sense and yet...

Today Lady Lucy had made perfect sense to her as well, hiding there in her bed in a darkened room where no one could get to her. She had stopped eating. She had ceased to want to live. The anger in Belle surfaced with a suddenness that she did not conceal.

Everyone was lying.

Her aunt.

Lady Lucy.

Even the handsome Earl of Thornton with his succession of mistresses and his bitter mother.

Taking leave of her aunt and walking to her own room, Belle lifted up a paintbrush, dipping it in oil and mixing it with red powder after finding a sheet of paper.

Nothing was real. Everything was false. She liked the banal deceiving strokes she drew as they ran across the truth and banished it. Lives built on falsity. Paintings borne on fury. Lady Lucy was young and well brought up. Belle wanted to kill the man who had left her the wreck that she was, but as yet there could be only the small and quiet steps of acceptance before the healing began.

Lytton spent the afternoon entwined in the arms of the beautiful widow Mrs Susan Castleton in the rooms he had provided for her in Kensington.

She had impeccable taste, he would give her that, but what had been wonderful, even as recent as last week, now was not.

His mother's words had stung and the look on Miss Annabelle Smith's face had stung further.

Why did the healer have to be so damned unusual? His sister had gulped down the broth and the crust and asked for a cup of tea to finish her lunch with. She had not eaten properly in weeks and now after a ten-minute visit with the contrary Miss Smith she was suddenly pulling herself out of the mire. Lucy thought she was a witch and had told him so, a woman of fearful evil and unspeakable power. She did not wish for her to visit again.

Well, if a witch could cajole his sister into rejoining the real world then so be it, and her alchemy would certainly be welcome in his town house after the disappointing efforts of all the other renowned physicians. He would be asking her back.

'You are so very well formed, Thornton.' The whisper in his ear had him turning, Susan's chestnut curls trailing across his chest when she tweaked his nipple, her body nudging his own in further invitation.

God, she was insatiable. When he had first met her he could barely believe his luck, but now…now he wondered if she might squeeze all the life from him and leave him as much a wreck as his sister.

'I want to eat you up. All of you.'

Her words were so like what he had just been thinking that he pushed her from him and sat up.

He didn't want this any more, this salacious liaison so far away from what he knew to be right. Even a few weeks ago he would have found such passion exciting. Now all he wanted to do was escape.

'I need to go, Susan. I am not sure if I shall be back.'

If this was too brutal for her then he was sorry for it, but he disliked lying. To anyone.

'You joke, surely, Thornton. We have been here all afternoon feeding off one another.'

The further reference to food made him stand and find his clothes. Fumbling with the one ring he wore today, he twisted it from his finger.

'It is worth the price of the rent on this place for at least another year. I thank you for your patience with me, but now it is finished. I can't do this any more.'

Tears began to fall down her cheeks. 'You cannot possibly be serious, Thornton. I love you, I love you with all my heart and—'

He stopped her by placing a finger across her generous reddened lips.

'You loved Derwent a year ago and you loved Marcus Merryweather before that. There will be another after me.'

As he walked away, garments in hand, she picked up a vase and threw it at him hard, the glass smashing against the side of his head and drawing blood as it shattered.

'You will regret this, I swear it. No one will ever make love to you in the way I have, especially one whom you might take as a wife. They are all cold and wooden and witless.'

Hell. Had Aurelian or Edward said something publicly of his plans to be married before the end of the Season? He hoped not. If that happened he would have a hundred mamas and their chicks upon him, courting him with guile and hope.

The day that had begun strangely just seemed to get stranger. He could feel warm blood running across one cheek and yet he couldn't go home because his mother was prowling through the corridors of his town house and Lucy had spent almost the entire morning crying.

His younger brother was in trouble again with his school and Prudence, his oldest sister, was in Rome seeing the sights with her new husband. He would have liked to talk with her, but she was not due back for at least a few months, skipping out of England with a haste that was unbecoming.

No one in his entire family was coping. His father's death the Christmas before last had seen to that and here he was, bogged down by the responsibility of a title he'd little reason to like and a mistress who had just tried to kill him.

Once he had been free and unburdened. Now every man and his dog wanted a piece of him. Once the most reading he had done was to glance at the IOUs from the gambling tables where his luck never seemed to run out. Now it was writing reports, filling out forms and doing all the myriad other things a large and complicated estate required.

He had barely come up for air in weeks save

in the bed of Susan Castleton, but that was now also lost to him. He couldn't regret this even a bit, he thought, as he finished dressing and made his leave.

He'd spend the evening at White's and when the place closed he'd go to Edward Tully's town house. At least Derwent would understand his fading interest in a woman whom he, too, had once been intimate with.

'You need to go abroad, Thorn, and escape your family.' Edward's words were said with the edge of strong cognac upon them.

'Easy for you to say with your father still hale and hearty and an older brother who will take on the heavy mantle of the title.'

Edward laughed as he upended yet another glass of cognac and gestured to a servant going by to bring another bottle. 'How are the marriage plans going?'

Lytton swore.

He'd confided in Lian and Edward about his intention to marry as a result of Lucy's ill health, his own mortality staring him in the face. He now wished he hadn't.

'Wide hips and a passable face wasn't it?' Edward plainly saw a humour that Lytton himself did not. 'The first girl you saw with both qualifications?'

'I was drunk.'

'More drunk than you are tonight?'

At that Lytton laughed. 'More drunk and also happier, possibly.'

'Well, Lian is happy and so is Shay. Perhaps a wife is the answer. A woman of substance. No shallow-brained ingénue or experienced courtesan.'

'And where are those women?' Lytton asked. 'Shay found Celeste in the underbelly of Napoleon's Paris and Lian's Violet was thrown up from the greed of treason and lost gold.'

'Stuart Townsend said he saw you this morning in a carriage with a woman he did not recognise, Thorn. He said she looked interesting?'

Lytton shook his head. For some reason he did not want to talk of Annabelle Smith. His whole family must have disappointed her today and he did not wish to continue the trend. He stayed silent.

'And the fact that you will not speak of her makes it even more interesting.'

He stood. 'I think I need to go home, Edward, and sleep. For a hundred years, if I only could.'

'There's a masked ball at the Seymours' tomorrow evening. Come with me to that and blow away a few cobwebs.'

'Perhaps I might. I will send you word in the morning.'

Outside the sky was clearer and the stars were out. A vibrant endless heaven, Lytton thought, enjoying the fresh air. He had meant to stay at Edward's, but suddenly wanted to be home.

Annabelle Smith was due tomorrow again at the ungodly hour of nine and he did not want to miss seeing her. That thought worried him more than any other.

Chapter Three

This morning Belle did not take her basket. Instead she brought a book, tied in blue ribbon and inscribed. Rose stayed at home.

The Earl of Thornton was waiting for her in the entrance hall when she arrived at his town house. Today there was no other servant present and he took her coat and hat himself and hung them on the brass pegs to one side of the front door.

A gash across his temple was the first thing she noticed.

'You have been hurt?'

'Barely,' he answered and swiped at his untidy fringe.

'It looks like more than that to me, your lordship.'

'Your patient is upstairs, Miss Smith.'

She smiled at the rebuke. 'And your mother?'

'Is behaving in her room.'

'Did your sister eat anything yesterday?'

'More than she has in weeks. She imagines you to be of the occult. A blooded witch, I think it was she called you.'

'There is strength in such imagination.'

At that he laughed out loud and dipped into his pocket. A ten-pound note lay in his palm. 'For you. You have done more in fifteen minutes for my sister than all the other physicians put together.'

'Oh, I could hardly take that much, your lordship. Ten pounds is a fortune and more than many people in Whitechapel might make in a whole year.'

'It is not for you, per se. I thought you told me yesterday you use your exorbitant fees for good in your parish.'

'I would and I do, but…'

He simply leaned forward to extract the velvet purse from the pocket of her coat on the peg and slid it inside before returning it. She could do nothing but concur.

'Thank you. I shall send you receipts for exactly what I have spent each penny upon. Your lordship.' She added this after a few seconds.

They had reached his sister's sitting room now, the place where Rose had waited yesterday, and he stopped.

'I think you would do better to see my sister alone today.'

Taking a breath, Belle nodded and went in.

This morning Lady Lucy was not hiding from her, but sitting in her bed gazing out of the window. She looked small and thin and pale.

'I hear you ate both lunch and dinner?'

The girl turned to her, anger in her eyes.

'As I am not used to being threatened, I deduced it good sense to eat something, Miss Smith. Just in case.'

'Then you would not mind if I read to you, either?' Pulling the ribbons from the book, Belle sat unbidden on the seat at the side of the bed and opened the first page.

Mary, the heroine of this fiction, was the daughter of Edward, who married Eliza, a gentle fashionable girl, with a kind of indolence in her temper which might be termed negative good nature...

* * *

Half an hour later she stopped.

'Who wrote this?'

Belle was heartened by the question. 'Mary Wollstonecraft. The writer truly believed that feminine imagination could transport women from cruel circumstance.'

Silence abounded, the tick of a clock in the corner all that could be heard in the room.

'I want to gift this book to you, Miss Staines. I hope we might discuss its possibilities next time I meet with you.'

'When would that be?'

'On Wednesday. That should allow you some time to come up with an opinion. An opinion I would value,' she added, seeing the dark uncertainty in golden eyes.

'I am not sure.'

'Eat and read, that is all I ask of you. Food for the body and for the mind.'

'How do you know my brother, the Earl of Thornton?'

'I don't, really.'

'Where did you meet him?'

'He came to my house in Whitechapel and asked me to visit you.'

'He paid you?'

'Very well. More than I am worth, probably.'

'Are you always so honest?'

'I find facing life head on is the best possible way of escaping difficulty.'

'My mother would not think that way.'

'Sometimes one needs to find confidence inside without being swayed by the influence of others.'

'You talk like Thorn. Do you know that? He cajoles everyone to do his bidding and he is so clever he can always find the words. Mama says he is like our father, but I do not think this is true. He is a thousand times better.'

'You love him?'

'Everyone does. But he is as unhappy as I am.'

Lord, this conversation was going in ways she had no idea of and Annabelle hoped with all her heart that the Earl of Thornton was not outside listening.

'Why are you so unhappy?'

The least she could do was to bring the focus back on her patient.

'I have become a mere nothing.'

The heroine's words from the book. Lady Lucy had been listening after all.

Belle lowered her voice. 'Motherhood is the furthest thing from nothing that I know of.'

Her patient started at that and blanched noticeably. 'Have you told him? My brother?'

'No.'

'Please do not. I need to think…'

With care Belle placed her hand across thin fingers. 'I give you my solemn oath that I shan't speak of your condition to anyone.'

'Thank you.'

When she looked away Belle rose, tucking the book into the folds of cloth on the bed so that it would not fall.

'I will see you on Wednesday.'

Outside she found Lytton Staines where she had left him, a drink in hand.

'I hope this visit will be as successful as your last.'

'I shall see your sister again next week, your lordship. There will be no payment required.'

'Miss Smith,' he said, a sound of exasperation in the word.

'Yes, your lordship.'

'I am an earl. Ten pounds is nothing at all to me and I shall pay you exactly what I think you are worth.'

'Are you made of money, then?' For a second he stood so close she could feel the whisper of his breath against her cheek as he replied.

'Yes.'

She almost liked his certainty and his arrogance at that moment. He was a man who valued honesty just as his sister had said and he was kind. Of all the attributes in people, that, to Annabelle, was the most important.

'I will also accompany you home.'

'It is not necessary. I am quite capable of getting myself back to Whitechapel.'

'I know you are, but I would like to see you safe.'

'Very well.'

She stepped back and he led the way downstairs, the wound on his left temple beginning to discolour. She would have offered to tend it, but something told her that he would decline such an invitation.

A rich man, a brother, a son, an earl. A man with mistresses and with enemies. A man of generosity and cleverness, too. So many things that she now knew of him as well as so many things she did not. She wondered just what he might think of her?

'Is my sister going to recover, do you think?'

He asked her this as the carriage slid away from the curb. Today it travelled slowly and she thought the Earl had had some hand in that, for he had been speaking with the driver just before they left.

Instead of answering his question she found one of her own. 'How did your father die?'

Her words were bare and shock ripped across his face.

'Why do you wish to know that?'

'Your sister said something that made me wonder.'

'What did she say?'

'She said that you were a thousand times better than he was.'

'Hell and damnation.'

She could not believe that she had heard the Earl swear in front of her and thought he might apologise for it, but instead he turned to look out of the window as he spoke again.

'He killed himself.'

He had asked her if she was a religious woman once and said that he did not put much stock in prayers. But she could see it did mean something, after all, for shock was etched on his face. He believed his father consigned to hell just as his sister did. A permanent banishment. An unchangeable tragedy.

'When did this happen?'

'Two Christmases ago. He gambled, you see, and lost. At least when I sit at the tables, I win.'

'What did he lose?'

'Balmain, the Thornton family estate. I got it back for him by the luck of a full flush a week later and he was not thankful.'

'The sins of the father are to be laid upon the children.'

'Words from the Bible?'

'And from William Shakespeare's *The Merchant of Venice.*'

'You are a mine of information, Miss Smith. From witchery or just plain and constant reading?'

'What do you think?' She couldn't add his title, not even if her life had depended on it, for here in the carriage there was a sort of equality that simmered between them and an energy that she had never felt with another.

'I think you watch people and listen with your heart.'

'You do that, too, my lord.'

This time he only smiled.

Belle steeped medicines and pounded tinctures and she charged nothing to a hundred patients who could afford very little. She brought warm clothing and blankets for the babies and she found packs of cards and puzzles for those with time to while away at the very endings of their lives. She paid for shoes that were not scuffed to within an inch of their existence and found oranges and fish fresh from the stalls in the market on Whitechapel Road. She noted down everything, every small and tiny charge, and sent the Earl of Thornton her reckoning two days before she was due to visit next.

Within an hour she had a message back.

That's the best ten pounds I have ever spent.

She was pleased for such an assurance. His handwriting was strong and flowing, the *b*'s and *p*'s were fluted in a way that made her smile. She brought the paper to her nose and breathed in, the scent of ink the only thing discernible.

What had she wanted it to smell like? Him?

Swallowing, she placed the note down carefully on her desk and crossed to the mirror, peering at herself once she was there.

She was not beautiful, nor perhaps even mildly pretty. Her hair was unremarkable and she had a tooth that did not sit at the same angle as the others. Her eyes were also far too blue to be restful.

She spoke well, she read widely and she helped others. These were her attributes. Searching her mind, she probed for the other distant truth that lay hidden well away from sense.

She wanted the Earl to like her. With more than respect. More than esteem. She was enough of a woman to have read the books on filial love, and on lust and on sexual endeavour. She had devoured *Fanny Hill* by John Cleland and read the compendium of poetry by the Earl of Rochester, clandestinely, under her bed sheets at night. The novel *Justine* had come into her hands through a bookseller in London for whom she had made medicines and she knew the erotic works of the Greek poets Strato and Sappho. She was no prude even if she was still a virgin.

But she was lonely.

She was also thirty-one, almost destitute, nameless, without family, and inclined to strange dreams at night that made her question her sanity come the morning.

The sum of being abandoned sat on her like a weight, altering worth and condemning certainty. No man had ever come near her in the way of a suitor. Did she repel them or was she simply repellent?

These thoughts of wanting more and wanting

it with a man like the Earl of Thornton were witless and unwise.

He had only ever looked at her in the way of an oddity, a woman who did not fit into any of the boxes the men of the *ton* needed their women to inhabit.

Appearance was not important to her and yet she was drawn to Lord Thornton's beautiful face with an ache. The wealth of a person was also a factor that had held no real weight. Yet the Earl's pounds had paid for things she would never have been able to procure otherwise, things that eased the wretched life of those struggling with very survival.

A conundrum and a puzzle.

She should take heed of his mother's warnings and make certain that she was soon gone from the lives of the Thorntons. Yet she couldn't. Lady Lucy needed her and, if truth be told, so perhaps did the Earl. To make him happier. To bring a smile across the sadness in his eyes.

They were right, these poets and novelists of long ago. The erotic hopes of a body were hot and heady things. Her hands ran across her breasts, nipples standing hard and proud.

She was not immune after all to the charms of men. No, she shook her head and rephrased. Not men, but one man. The enigmatic and beautiful Earl of Thornton. She knew it was stupid. But there it was. Unarguable.

Lytton smiled at the letter Annabelle Smith had sent him. Fish and stockings, blankets and coats were not things he usually read of, but each item here had been qualified with the person who had received it and that was what made it fascinating reading.

A young child with a chest complaint that was ongoing, a housewife pregnant for the eighth time in one of the winding and narrow alleys off the Whitechapel Road. An old soldier without a leg who was nearing sixty and needed a pack of cards to fill in the hours of a lonely day.

Numbers had always been simple things for him and if his father had squandered the coffers of the Thorntons', then he had refilled them ten times over. Easily. But these pounds that he had accrued also lacked depth, no story behind them save that of an investment.

His mother's voice brought him from his thoughts and he watched as she came into the room, a book in hand.

'Have you seen what your healer has left Lucy?'

He looked up and shook his head as the small tome with blue ribbons was delivered with force to his desk.

'Mrs Mary Wollstonecraft writes that men and women need educational equality and is critical of conventional women. If one were to believe in her premises, where would society be? Washed up, I tell you, each wife and mother attending to her own needs and not to those of her husband and her children. Books like this are a disgrace, Thornton, and one you need to be aware of and forbid when the insidious opinion comes beneath your own roof, crawling into your sister's consciousness.'

For a moment he looked at Cecelia and wondered when it was his mother had changed from a gentle parent into this one? The death of his father, he supposed. It could not have been easy for a woman who would listen so carefully to gossip.

'Perhaps returning to Balmain would be a good thing for you? Lucy's sickness has not been easy for any of us.'

'You cannot think I might leave her? My God, she is still at death's door.'

'I think we both know that is not true. She is eating again and her countenance is rosier. Certainly, we have passed the point of no return and Miss Smith has done wonders for her.'

'Wonders?' The word was whispered. 'It is witchcraft she has employed and who knows how long such things truly last?'

'Being grateful might bolster hope, Mama. Miss Smith is a woman who is an accomplished healer and there is no more to it than that.'

'She knows things.'

'Pardon?' Lytton looked up.

'Lucy says that she can read her mind and find out exactly what she is thinking. She says it is unsettling.'

'Yet she still wishes to meet her. She told me so this morning, so it cannot be too uncomfortable.'

'Your father would not have allowed it. Such a one in the house. He would have told her to leave the moment she tried to inveigle herself in to our family affairs and sent her packing back to Whitechapel where she belongs.'

'He is dead, Mama. And has been for a good year and a half.'

'Someone shot him. Someone broke into Balmain and shot him. I know it.'

For a second horror slid down the back of his neck. His mother was going mad and he had not noticed. How long had she been like this? He had been so busy trying to save the estate he had given his mother's mental state little thought but Lucy must have known as well as David and Prudence. No wonder his oldest sister had disappeared off abroad and his brother was playing up at school.

A tumbling house of cards, he ruminated, and walked across to Cecelia, taking her hand as he led her to a seat by the window.

'I want you to go back to the country. I will bring Lucy up in a week or two and spend some weeks there as well. You need to rest, for this has all been more than trying for you.'

Unexpectedly his mother nodded. 'Perhaps you are right. I could garden and tend to my flowers and walk a little. The glade is always beautiful at this time of the year. When Lucy returns we can follow quiet pursuits.'

Patting her hand, he was glad as she calmed. 'The carriage will be readied in the early afternoon and the family physician will accompany you just to be certain. Everything will be arranged so that you will not have to worry again and your great friend Isabel will be thrilled to have you back.'

After his mother had gone Lytton did another hour's work to see to all the details of her journey before picking up the book and wandering into Lucy's room. He found her up in an armchair that was slanted towards the sun. She wore a thick nightdress tied at the waist and her feet were bare.

'It is fine to see you up again.'

Her smile brightened when she noticed him and brightened further when she glanced at the book he was carrying. 'Mama took it away.'

He handed it back to her. 'The stuff of treason, she thinks.'

'What do you think?'

'I have not read it, but there are movements afoot to cast more light on the inequalities of women. A lot of it makes sense.'

She undid the blue ribbons and found a dog ear on the top of one page.

'Listen to this.'

With exaggerated care she read a few pages to him, her voice trembling with the tale of the woman she spoke of. When she had finished she placed the opened book on her breast and looked over at him.

'It is saying that women need to have their own opinions and they are just as valuable as any a man might have. The story is a sad one and one of deceit and lies as the heroine and her friend try to come to terms with their life in a madhouse. Miss Smith says she wants to hear my opinion on the trials of women when I see her next.'

'Well, it seems that you certainly hold one. Do you like Miss Smith?'

'I think at first she frightened me. But she is strong. She does not take nonsense easily.'

'Nonsense like witchcraft?'

'You have been speaking with Mama? I made

the mistake of telling her that perhaps Miss Smith was a witch when I first saw her and she took up this thought and would not stop speaking of it. I didn't realise how much anger she suddenly seems to be full of, though Prudence had warned me of it before she left.' She hesitated for a moment and then continued. 'I was wondering if I could ask Miss Smith to stay for morning tea when she comes. I know how busy she is, but the cook could make her famous scones and we have the raspberry jam from last year's crop at Balmain.'

'Of course. I won't need the carriage so she can be taken home in it afterwards.'

'Will you be here to join us?'

Lytton shrugged his shoulders. 'I have a meeting in the city which is important.'

'But if you can be here, would you?'

'I will try.'

In the afternoon Lytton visited the Thornton family banker and was reassured by the state of the finances. He knew the numbers himself, of course, but since attaining the Earldom he had been very careful to check every detail of his investments. He did not trust anyone.

He had a family to look after, thousands of acres of land to tend, servants and workers to provide for. The days of being careless were over, he had accepted that on the death of his father.

The keeping of a mistress was a lot less persuasive than it had once been as well. Susan Castleton had sent him copious notes trying to win back his favours, but he had replied to none of them.

He had heard from Edward how his name had been slandered by her in society, but that was the least of his worries. After the weeks of his sister being so sick, to have a glimmer of light in the future was gratifying and he did owe it to the unusual Miss Annabelle Smith.

Her vibrant blue eyes watched him in memory and for just a second he wondered what it would be like to have her beneath him tumbling into his bed.

The shock of that brought him to a standstill. There was no way in the world that he could enjoy her like that. The next woman he bedded would have to be his wife and she would need credentials and breeding that were incomparable to become a countess.

Still, the vision of Annabelle Smith naked with her dark curtain of hair falling around them was hard to shake off. Was she a virgin? Had she any experience with the pleasures of the flesh? God, even that thought had him hardening, here in the street with the daylight of London all about him and myriad shoppers walking past.

He could teach her everything he knew, every nuance of desire.

'Thorn.' The voice came through a haze and he turned to find Summerley Shayborne crossing the street to reach him.

'You look preoccupied.'

He smiled. 'I've just come from the bank.'

'Good news?' Shay knew of the trouble he'd been in last year with the estate when things had been turned upside down.

'Everything is fine and long may it stay that way.'

'You're the new and shining light of the financial world, I hear. An earl who seems to be able to pinpoint a lucrative investment without comparison? Most peers are holding on to the family plot by their fingernails, but it seems your latest project has just come through with flying colours.'

'The canning factory outside London? People need to eat and preserved fruit and vegetables are within the budget of most. Every large town in England by the end of the year will sport such a factory. Come in with me as a partner. I'll get Lian and Edward on board as well.'

'You're serious?'

'I am.'

'When can we draw up the contracts?' Shay looked excited.

'Next week. But keep it quiet for I don't want someone else beating me to the post.'

'Have a drink with us now, then. Celeste is at the town house and we would love your company.'

'Very well.' He hailed his carriage and they both piled in.

Lytton had always admired Shay's wife. She was tough in a way that intrigued him and beautiful enough to take his breath away every time he saw her.

She also was nothing like the bride that the *ton* had thought the lauded Summerley Shayborne, Viscount Luxford, would choose for himself.

'You said you would come to Luxford in the early summer, Thorn, but you didn't.' Celeste looked puzzled.

'I've been at Balmain for quite a few weeks because my sister has been sick. We have only just returned to town.'

'I've heard that just lately she is making some sort of a recovery?'

'I hope so. I have engaged a healer to try to coax her out of bed where she has been languishing. Miss Annabelle Smith from Whitechapel is her name and she seems to be making quite a difference.'

'The herbalist? She is the woman my lady's maid was speaking of so highly the other day, Summer. I should very much like to meet her. Is she at your town house this week seeing your sister?'

'Tomorrow she is, but only very early. At nine. She keeps unusual hours.'

'Could we call in? It might be my only chance to talk with the woman and she sounds more than fascinating.'

'Well, I don't see why not.'

Lytton had organised a meeting for the morning, but he supposed he could cancel it. His thoughts from earlier on had not left him and he felt...anxious. He could not quite imagine Annabelle Smith chatting about things with his sister and Celeste over jam scones and a cup of tea. He wondered, too, if Celeste had read any of the writings of Mary Wollstonecraft?

It was her birthday.

Well, her birthday as Tante Alicia had deemed it given she was four when she had turned up in the French village without any past whatsoever.

The third of July. A hot morning in the village of Moret-sur-Loing when a nun had delivered a sick child to the house of the local healer and pleaded for the girl to be taken in.

This much she did know for Alicia had retold

this story over and over and never a mention of the people who had abandoned her.

Annabelle had celebrated today with a new pair of stockings and a fresh orange. She had also fashioned her hair a little differently this morning, doing away with the heavy scarf and pinning it about her face. The curls escaped, of course, but rather than detracting from the whole picture she thought that they added to it. For some reason today she felt lighter and happier than she had in months and the sun above was a part of that, too.

She hoped Lady Lucy had read the book she had given her. She hoped she had kept eating, too. If she had, then the change in her from last week to this one should be more than noticeable.

A carriage standing before the Thornton town house had Belle frowning. She did not recognise it and hoped that there were not visitors who would take away time she would have with the Earl's sister. The horses were most handsome and the liveried driver on the box seat tipped his hat at her.

'Morning, miss. It's a fine day outside, to be sure.'

She smiled back at him and made her way up the steps, the door opened by a servant she had not met before.

'The master is expecting you, miss. He is in the blue salon. I will take you through.'

Dispensing with her coat and hat, she followed him and heard the conversation between a group of people getting louder by the moment.

She stopped and the servant looked around.

'I think there has been a mistake. I am here to see Miss Staines only. I have been attending to her medical needs.'

'You are Miss Smith, are you not?'

'Yes.'

'Well then, you are to come right this way.'

Belle straightened down her skirts as she went, a sort of dawning horror rising in her stomach. She did not wish to meet other guests of this house. She would not be accepted by anyone in society and surely the Earl of Thornton would know this.

The door opened. The Earl stood by the mantel with two strangers, a beautiful woman and a tall and handsome man. When the Earl saw her he excused himself and came to her side.

'I thought before you went upstairs to see my sister you may like to meet Lord and Lady Luxton.'

Belle took in a breath. This was a situation she had not come across before and she was silent as she watched for cues.

'Miss Smith.' The woman spoke first. 'I am Celeste Shayborne and I have heard much about your ministry in Whitechapel. My husband is most interested in hearing about it, too.'

As if to underline this as a truth the man beside her nodded.

'It seems your fame proceeds you, Miss Smith.' Lord Luxford spoke now for the first time, though Belle wondered at his tone. He did not sound quite as pleased as his wife. The social conventions worried her.

Should she curtsy before this lord as she spoke or was that unnecessary?

'Mine is a small clinic but in an area where there are many supplicants. I am quite perplexed that you have even heard of it.'

* * *

She used her voice like a weapon, Lytton thought, the low and husky tone surprising, but not as surprising as the King's English that she now spoke. Her voice had never held tones of the East End, though, and had always sounded quite refined.

If he had closed his eyes just then, it could have been any one of the titled and well-brought-up ladies of the *ton* talking. He saw the interest in Celeste's eyes and the curiosity in Shay's.

'Who are your parents, Miss Smith?' Celeste was never one to refrain from trying to decipher a puzzle and she asked the question baldly.

But Miss Annabelle Smith failed to answer, turning to him instead and finding a query all her own.

'I do hope your sister has recovered a little in the days since I have seen her, your lordship?

Now this was interesting, Lytton thought. There were secrets here and he could tell that Celeste had determined it exactly the same.

'Miss Smith gave Lucy a copy of the Mary Wollstonecraft book, Celeste, and my sister has been most taken by the things the author wrote of.'

'Oh, I, too, have read her books and most heartily agree with the sentiments in them.'

Belle did not feel quite up to arguing for the rights of all women no matter what their station in life so she stayed quiet. She was feeling her way here and the truth of her being from Whitechapel's mean streets felt like an enormous stumbling block. She had not recognised this in the company of the Earl or even of his sister. But when society came crashing down upon her in a refined drawing room as it had here there was no getting away from it.

She did not fit.

A headache had begun to form behind her eyes and she prayed to God that the jagged lines of a worse malady did not reappear. Not until she could get home at least. She felt sweat run between her breasts and the fine beading of it on her top lip.

The Earl saved the day by asking her if she wanted a drink, leading her across to a cabinet where an array of bottles stood on top of a polished mahogany counter.

She had never tasted true liquor in all of her life and searched for something non-alcoholic.

'The white wine is very good.' The Earl lent down and said this quietly.

'Only a small glass, please.'

He poured it with the sort of ease people used to heavy drinking must be wont to do. She did not really know, for her aunt was a teetotaller and any alcohol in the house was reserved for medicines. The devil's brew, her aunt had often said, and there was enough evidence around Whitechapel for them to believe in such a truth.

A cup of tea would have been welcome, but she felt she could not ask. The smile she sported hurt her cheeks and she wondered how much longer she could manage to keep it up. She wished she might excuse herself and go upstairs to see her patient.

'Celeste and Shay are friends of mine.'

'I see, your lordship.'

'Very good friends.'

She looked up and caught his glance. What

did he wish her to say? And what was he telling her?

The tumble of the unexpected was confusing, terrifying even, and she measured her breaths with a rigid count. These people knew of her and her clinic, they understood she was from poorer stock and they were still attempting to be friendly. She took a sip of the wine and then another, surprised by the strength of its taste.

Still, it was wet and it gave her something to do. In a moment she had finished the lot.

'Would you like more?' A frown dashed into golden eyes as she nodded.

'Thank you.'

This time she drank more slowly as he led her back into the room. It was relaxing her now, this white wine. For the first time in ten minutes she felt as if she might be coping.

'Where did you learn your healing skills, Miss Smith?'

Celeste Shayborne's voice had the lilt of another country in the words. French, perhaps. She recognised the cadence.

'My aunt is a herbalist. She taught me.'

'It must take a long time to learn?'

'Years and years. I am still learning now and Tante Alicia is sixty-three and she says she does not know it all yet either. She has tried her hardest to teach me, though, in the hope that such knowledge will not be lost and I could be the one to hand it down to the next generation.'

Goodness. Had she said too much? She tried to remember every word she had uttered and found that she couldn't, a barrier between her and the world.

It was the wine. Placing her near-empty glass down on a table, she wished again that she could have asked for tea or coffee, anything to neutralise the rising warmth that was worrying.

Control was slipping and with it reserve.

'Your aunt is French?' Celeste Shayborne clapped her hands. 'Do you speak the language?'

'A little,' she said before she thought, for Lytton Staines had heard her using it on that very first day they had met after Stanley had torn his waistcoat. He would know that what she said was a lie, but she did not want the next questions that might rise with such an honesty.

The Earl's voice broke her panic and she was pleased for his words.

'I think something non-alcoholic might be useful.' He poured a large glass of lemonade and handed it over.

Relief flooded into panic. She would be all right now. She would manage.

Exhaustion swamped gratitude and then sadness overcame that. So many emotions in so very few seconds she could hardly keep up. If she were at home she would lie down with a pillow across her head to keep out the daylight and she would sleep until the headache left her. Sometimes she took sulphate of quinine if it were severe, or cinchona bark or valerian. But there was nothing here that was remotely like anything she needed. She could see Celeste Shayborne looking at her with a frown in her eyes and even the Earl gave the impression of worry.

'I am quite all right. It's only a headache and I have them all the time. The wine was strong, too, and it's still early in the morning...'

A further glance from Thornton told her that her admission had been unexpected, inappropriate even, and her words tailed off. Shaking her head, she tried hard to find a balance.

'Perhaps on reflection I might be wise to leave. It seems that today is not a good day and I think I may need to go home and sleep.'

Another faux pas and had she just spoken completely in French?

'I think my headache is worsening and when that happens I am never good company.'

Goodness, now she was switching languages, the words blurring into each other, skipping over tenses and trailing into gibberish. She could not be quite sure she had pronounced any of them properly.

'So I bid you au revoir.' She had not seen Lady Lucy as she had promised, but did not feel at all up to it. She would come back tomorrow when she felt she might manage.

The Earl's arm was around her waist now and she allowed him to lead her to the door. Once in the entrance hall he found her hat and coat and then took her out to the carriage that he had asked to be brought around. Inside the conveyance, cocooned in silence and the comfort of the squashy leather seats, she breathed out.

'I am sorry.'

'For what.'

'For creating a spectacle. For being vulgar.'

'I hardly think you were that, Miss Smith. Entertaining is more the word that comes to mind.'

'You are kind.'

'Often in life I am not.'

She ignored that. 'Your friends were kind, too.'

'Have you ever drunk wine before?'

'No.'

'God.' His laughter was not quite what she expected.

'I hope as a consequence you don't want your ten pounds back now for I have spent it already.'

'I know of that. You sent me a note, remember. I did not realise that small sum of money could purchase so much. I commend you, Miss Smith.'

'Belle.'

'Pardon.'

'Belle. You can call me that. Everyone else does. It means beautiful in French, but I do not think she should have named me such for I am not.'

'Hell.'

'You are swearing again, my lord Earl. I'm not sure you should. It is more than rude and, while I am not a high-born lady, I am still a woman.'

He knocked on the window and the conveyance stopped. 'Take the long road around London for at least an hour, Barnes, and stop at the next shop that sells lemonade.'

'Lemonade, my lord?'

'In a very large bottle.'

Chapter Four

She had gone to sleep on his shoulder, her head pushed against him and one hand lying in his lap. His fine embroidered jacket was creased and the hat he had worn was on the floor beside him. Outside the day looked a lot later than it should have been.

'What time is it?' she asked, jerking away with horror. Her mouth felt furry and her stomach nauseous.

'Half past twelve.'

'We have stopped?'

'The horses needed a rest from walking.'

'Oh, my God.' She placed her head in her hands and said it again. 'You are telling me that we have been driving around London because I fell asleep? This is worse than Stanley, worse than the waistcoat, worse even than my trying to clean you up...' Trailing off, she groaned again before relapsing into silence.

'I think you exaggerate, Miss Smith. Nothing could ever be worse than a torn pink waistcoat.'

She laughed because there was nothing else for it and because she was grateful for his humour.

'I think it was the wine. Could you give your friends my apologies? I doubt that I shall ever see them again, but still...' She looked at him then and a new shame washed across her.

'Shay has worked as a spy in the war-torn countries of Europe and Celeste has been there along with him. They are not shrinking violets, Miss Smith, and I think a laugh is good for everybody.'

'You were reassuring me until the very last line, your lordship, and what of your sister's needs? As her healer I am supposed to be responsible and above reproach?'

He laughed again. 'And who is ever that in a whole lifetime?'

'Not me.'

'Put it behind you, Miss Smith, and decline the wine next time. Perhaps you are a lush?'

'A what?'

'A person for whom wine is intoxicating? I have never seen anyone get drunk quite so quickly before and on so little.'

'Oh, God.' Now remorse was back.

How awful had she been? How uncontrolled? She could recall pieces only in snatches. Large parts of the past few hours had gone, but the Earl's last memory of her would always be this.

He wore only one gold ring today and the wound at his temple was largely healed. She took in the small details of him piece by piece with an avid hope. The hope that every tiny shred of him might be recalled later to make her smile or wish for more, for so very much more.

Time. Words. Laughter. Life. As potent as any medicine she administered and as useful. That touch of truth had her turning towards him, the back of her hand resting against his all the way down the Whitechapel Road. She liked the warmth of it.

'My God, Thorn, who is Miss Smith and where the hell did you find her?'

Shay had arrived back at his town house late that same evening, the moon slight and the night dark.

Lytton leant back in his chair, sending up a plume of smoke from the cheroot before him. Around him his house had settled. Lucy had recovered from her fury over Miss Smith leaving early, retiring on the promise that he would contact her come morning and arrange a further meeting. His mother had departed yesterday for Balmain so that distraction was gone and Susan Castleton had finally ceased to hound him hourly about reigniting the dead flame of their disastrous affair.

All in all it was good to sit and consider his day, quietly.

'Annabelle Smith is not as she seems,' he replied. 'There are secrets that she holds close, but I do not know of them. Yet.'

'Celeste loved her. She is sending Miss Smith an invite to spend some time with us at Luxford. Do you think she might come?'

'Probably not.' Lytton refilled both their glasses. 'By her own account she seldom leaves the borders of Whitechapel. Even Portman Square was a stretch.'

'A mystery, then, and one that refuses to un-ravel?'

'I think she unravelled completely this morn-ing, don't you?'

'Did you accompany her back to Whitecha-pel?'

'No, not for a while. I took her on a carriage ride around London until she sobered up. She went to sleep and I waited with her on the far side of Hyde Park. Three hours later we man-aged to return her home.'

'It just gets more and more interesting,' Shay said and began to laugh.

'What does?'

'That you should be protecting her as you do. Is she your mistress?'

'Hell. What do you think?'

'I don't know what to think, that is the trou-ble. She looks like a sultry angel, gets drunk like a sot and speaks two languages, both in the accents of the high born. And yet she resides in Whitechapel? There has to be a story there.'

'Don't dig, Shay. I want her to tell me of it herself.'

'There you go again. Who have you turned into, Thorn? I have never before known you to be so protective of a woman and one you imply you are not even sleeping with. Every unmarried female of the *ton* would like you to place a wedding ring on their finger and the unhappily married ones would settle for merely a turn in your bed. You have thrown off Mrs Castleton and made a fortune with every investment that you touch, yet here you are...shepherding a secretive seraph around London and keeping her well away from the wolves of society.'

'Perhaps there is still some slight bit of decency left in me then, after all?'

'Or perhaps you have finally met your match?'

'Enough, Shay. Let's have a drink and talk business. It seems at least then we might agree on the facts that are before us.'

Hours later when Shay had gone Lytton walked to the window and looked out over the streets of London. He turned towards the east. Miss Belle Smith would be there, stewing medicines and chopping plants, the dog Stanley watching her even as a hundred dangers hung around just outside her door. He wished she were here in Portman Square, safe and warm. He wished her hand still sat next to his own, the touch of her filling up his whole body with joy.

He wanted to gift her with as many pounds as she needed for her ragtag group of patients, but he did not dare to mention it for she didn't look like a woman who would take well to charity.

She was prickly and wise and innocent and unusual. She was also completely herself. He smiled, liking that assessment more than all the others put together.

He would call in tomorrow to see whether she would deign again to visit his sister, this time with the promise of only that. He sincerely hoped that she might say yes, not so much for Lucy's sake but for his own.

Rosemary Greene helped her to strip away the skin from the aloes and pulverise the green squashy middle of the plant for an ointment she had found very effective in the treatment of burns.

'You seem quiet, Belle?'

'I had a headache yesterday and I always feel slightly heavy afterwards.'

'The Earl brought you home in his carriage? Alicia mentioned it and so did every other inhabitant living in this corner of Whitechapel.'

Annabelle decided to be honest. 'I think I got a little drunk, Rose. He poured me two glasses of wine and I swallowed them quickly. I should not have.'

'Goodness. Does your aunt know?'

She shook her head. 'Please don't tell her of it. It was my fault.'

'And the Earl, was he honourable?' A stillness fused into each word.

'He was. He sat with me in the carriage while I slept and then accompanied me home.'

'Did he touch you?'

'Only on the hand. He was by no means offensive.'

Rose returned to the task of wetting the aloe. 'Men can take advantage of innocence, Belle. They are not always principled. You have to be most careful, especially around gentlemen of wealth for they are the very worst.'

A sudden vision of Lady Lucy being pressured into something she did not want made Annabelle stand up. She needed to go back and talk with the Earl's sister.

She wondered how she might see her without having to go through the Earl of Thornton. The idea of a letter was the most appealing, but she could not be such a coward.

Stanley was barking again at the front door, an incessant noise reverberating through the house. She loved the small terrier, but sometimes he was a handful and today she just did not feel like listening to such a ruckus.

'I will put him in with Alicia,' she told Rose, wiping her hands and then grabbing the dog by his collar. After seeing Stanley banished, she passed the front door again and noticed a shadow glimmering against the small window to one side. Someone was here? A patient? She was not expecting anyone this morning and hoped it was not an emergency.

Opening the door, she found the Earl of Thornton about to knock. He was dressed today in riding clothes and when she peered out she saw another man there holding two horses, his dress much the same.

'Good morning, Miss Smith. My sister has sent me to your doorstep on the express condition that I ask if there would be a possibility of spending some time just with her tomorrow. She is far better than she was, but is most distressed at missing you yesterday. If I sent the Thornton carriage tomorrow afternoon at two, would that be suitable for you?'

Belle could barely believe he was here as she nodded her head. He had not sent her a written message or dispatched a servant to do his bidding, but had come himself and in full glory at half past ten in the morning?

'Lucy also bade me tell you that there will be tea and scones. The jam is raspberry from a particularly good batch in Balmain this past summer.'

'Then I can't see how I might refuse, your lordship.'

'You like raspberries?'

'I do.'

When he smiled the light danced in his eyes and the sun caught the gold of his hair and her breath hitched. There were a number of people on the street outside who watched him, but he did not seem to notice them as he tipped his hat and left. Shutting the door behind him, Belle leaned against it.

His formal visit held the same emotion as yesterday and, standing here in an old apron over an even older gown, she could not understand why. Her hands were still green from the aloe and her hair was roughly bundled into an untidy knot. The visage and clothes of the beautiful Lady Luxford shimmered in her memory, a woman of class and dignity. A woman who would not get drunk in a drawing room in the early hours of the morning and then virtually fall over on her face on the way to the door.

Everything had been simpler before she had met the Thorntons. Her business had been growing and she had felt a certain pride in what she had achieved. But now…now Lady Lucy's dreadful secret gnawed at her happiness and the Earl's very presence rattled her composure.

Thirty-two was not an age to be so very unsettled. She needed to see to the future of the Earl of Thornton's sister and then never visit either of them again. A loss bloomed at this thought, but she pushed it away quickly as she went inside to help Rose.

An invitation to the Derwent Ball was one of the most sought-after tickets of the Season. The Earl of Derwent, Patrick Tully, and his wife, Priscilla, always went to such extremes in decorating their salons and the food and music was renowned.

Lytton had come tonight because Edward Tully was a close friend and because he needed some distraction from all that was happening with Lucy. He also needed to stop thinking of Miss Annabelle Smith.

Everyone was there, the crush of success stopping him in his tracks as he filed through the front door in the company of Edward Tully.

'My God, it gets busier every year, Ed.'

'My brother will be pleased. He puts a lot into it.'

'And you?'

'I'm thinking of heading for the Americas, Thorn, to get away for a while.'

'And do what?'

'I could start up one of those canning factories you are always talking of. New York sounds like a big enough city and you've already asked me to be a partner.'

'If you are serious, I'd like you to be involved.' He turned to look at Edward and realised he looked a lot less than happy.

'I want more from life, Lytton. I want adventure and surprise. Come with me. We could both do with a break, I think.'

'I can't. Not now.'

'Because of Lucy?'

Lytton shook his head. Lucy was finally making a recovery, but the face of Miss Smith came to mind. He did not want her to be so alone.

'Hell.' He swore as he saw Susan Castleton bearing down upon him, forgetting everything except the overriding desperation to escape.

Edward comprehending his unease, shuffled him sideways into a group standing near the door. Albert Tennant-Smythe, Lord Huntington, was one of the men there and Lytton's ire rose. He had never liked Tennant-Smythe, his brash confidence founded on putting others down. Barely acknowledging him, he felt the anger reciprocated even as Huntington excused himself and left.

Odd that, he thought. Usually the fellow was so much more in your face and he also knew he was interested in becoming a part of his investment in the fruit and vegetable cannery production.

Lady Beatrice Mallory next to him had begun to talk and he leaned down to listen to what she said through all the noise.

'I saw Lady Luxford yesterday afternoon, my lord, and she said your sister was much recovered.'

'She is.'

'It seems you have inveigled the mysterious healer from Whitechapel to visit her and she has conjured up wonders. Lady Luxford was full of her praise. I remember seeing your sister at the Vauxhall Gardens a few months ago in the company of Huntington and his friends and she looked beautiful.'

The first niggle of something not being quite right took him by surprise. Why the hell would Lucy have been with that group, the wild arrogance of a set who took no care of others, concerning him. He had heard no word of such an excursion and he was certain his mother would not have encouraged it.

Nothing tonight was allowing him comfort. In honesty all he wanted was to be back in his carriage, ferrying a sleeping Miss Smith around the quieter roads of London and feeling the warmth of her hand against his own. That thought worried him, too. Was he going as mad as his mother? He took a glass of brandy offered by a passing footman and drank it quickly. He needed oblivion and he needed it fast. It had been a long time since he had been truly drunk, but tonight even the thought of it helped.

An hour later he found himself at the card tables, Albert Tennant-Smythe opposite him.

'The stakes are high, Thornton, but I hear you are well heeled these days so it should not bother you.'

'What are you putting on the table?'

'An Arabian thoroughbred.'

'Your horse?'

'My grandmother's.'

'She'll be happy to lose it?'

'Deal the cards, Thornton, and spit up the money if you are man enough.'

It was almost too easy to win and even with a good deal of brandy under his belt Lytton wondered at the method of the others' card counting.

Within twenty moments he had an IOU for the steed and there was a crowd of interested onlookers around them. Albert Tennant-Smythe looked furious and it was only the good sense of the Derwents to have provided hired muscle in the card rooms that saved a fight. Three burly boxers escorted Huntington from the house, his howls demanding another round drowned by the laughter of those in the room.

'You want to lose every other horse you don't own as well?'

'We will see what your grandmother might have to say about that.'

'This loss will be a thorn in Huntington's side, mark my words.'

Lady Huntington, the Dowager Countess, was known for her steel hand in trying to give guidance to progeny without moral integrity and Albert was the only grandchild still living.

Personally Lytton thought the ending of a family line with so little going for it might be a good thing and pitied any bride who would attach all her hopes to a man who'd probably never live up to them.

Lady Beatrice Mallory's words were also in the mix. Why the hell would Lucy have been in Tennant-Smythe's company? Tomorrow he would ask her and offer his advice to stay well away from a troublemaker for whom he held no liking.

He would see what else he could find out about Huntington in the meantime, who his friends were and what was the structure of his family ties. There was the grandmother, of course, but were there others, too, who it might be wise to understand more about.

Lytton had always trusted his instincts and he had a bad feeling about the Earl.

Belle took Lucy's hand and stroked her fingers, a plate of scones and a cup of tea beside her.

'You need to talk to your brother about your condition. You need his help.'

'Why? If I tell him everything, Thorn will insist on marriage and there is no way at all that I would ever want that.'

'Did he hurt you physically when…?' She could not go on.

'No. I went with him willingly because I thought he was dashing, I suppose, until I really knew what he was like and by then it was too late.'

'You said that he was years older than you are and as such he should have known better. Would you want me to talk to him?'

'I don't know. Would he listen?'

'I'd make him.'

Lucy began to laugh. 'How?'

'Let me think about that. I won't do anything at all until I speak to you. Would that be something you would be happy with?' Putting out her hand, Belle was glad when the young girl placed her own within it.

'Don't say anything to Thorn, though. I need to get a bit stronger before I can deal with all of this yet and the last year and a half has not been an easy one for our family.'

'What of your sister? Prudence, is it?'

'She is in Rome with her husband. She is also eight years older than I am and hasn't much time to listen to my opinions.'

'And your mother?'

'You saw what she is like. Papa's death has changed her and she is bitter now. Poor Thorn has had to deal with all of that as well as an errant younger brother and a bankrupt Earldom. He won back our country seat in a game of cards just before our father died. Did you know that?'

'From whom?'

'I am not certain as he has never talked of it and it would be poor form to mention it anywhere else. My brother has the Midas touch in business though, and lately has been turning preserved food into gold.'

'Preserved food?'

'He has one big canning factory not far from London with more popping up all across England. Most everyone can afford a can of preserves and that is where the money lies.'

Belle could hear those exact words coming from the Earl of Thornton's lips.

'He will marry soon, though, and I suppose

to a wife who won't like us. She will be beautiful and cold and well born and then Thorn will become distant and we will all have to move out.'

'What makes you say that?'

'Because that is what happens in families of the *ton* and ours is falling apart at the seams. What bride would truly want to deal with us?' She straightened the bedcover as she said this, smoothing the quilt down. 'There are many in society who would vie for his hand. I've had to listen to small confessions from women about their penchant for my brother for months now. There is one woman, Lady Catherine Dromorne, whom people are touting as the next Countess. Our families are friends.'

Belle looked around Lucy's room. The decor was beautiful and tasteful and expensive. Every single bit of this house screamed money, from the manicured gardens to the tiled roof top. Nothing looked old or scuffed or mediocre. The Earl's Countess would presumably be exactly the same, a woman of refinement and breeding and pride.

The exact opposite of her.

'He left his mistress, Mrs Castleton, just recently, but she has been hounding him to come back.'

Annabelle hardly knew what to say to this.

'Lady Catherine has been a particular friend of his for a long while and Mama always imagined they might marry, but...'

When Lucy tailed off Belle felt regret. There was no one else in her world who could tell her anything of Lord Thornton's personal affairs and all Lucy's revelations were eye openers. When she had talked of her seduction by a man nearly twice her age it was all that Belle could do to hold in the anger she trembled with. Lord Huntington would get his dues, she promised, for there were many in Whitechapel who would jump at the chance to go with her to visit him. Big men, rough men. A threat would be enough, she was sure. Not to force him to marry Lucy, that was the last thing she wanted, but to get him to apologise. There was a healing in an apology and a properly felt and expressed one would go a long way in allowing Lady Lucy to move on with her life. She hoped he might cry a little, this despicable Lord. A well-aimed punch to the stomach would probably elicit some tears, but it could be nothing that showed. Lady Lucy needed to believe in his repentance even if she herself never would.

Men like him did not change their spots. No, they went on to grimmer and grimmer crimes and she pitied anyone who had to weather that ride. She had seen this a number of times in Whitechapel. The desperate wives and mothers worrying if every day that their wayward son or husband lived might be their last. Happiness was not that golden easy glow that the stories talked of. It was the small satisfactions that came in tiny victories. A loaf of bread that was not mouldy. A shilling over at the end of a long hard week. A child who recovered quickly from a cough that had been worrying. A husband who returned home late after a fight, a little worse for wear, but still alive.

The Thorntons were immune in some ways to tragedy and exposed to it in other ways. Lady Lucy's innocence had counted against her just as her brother's success and arrogance had counted against him.

His sister would not take him into her confidence. Belle was pleased, at least, that the girl had spoken to her about what had happened for there was a release in confession.

Her pregnancy would be almost eight or nine weeks along. Soon it would show. Already there were times when she caught the red cheeks of expectancy and the curves that were softening. But Thornton was no fool. He would not be hoodwinked for much longer, either, and when he knew that Belle had not confided in him there would be hell to pay.

The Earl was the one doling out for her services and when he asked her for a diagnosis for his sister which she knew he would, she would have to lie.

'I think that Mrs Wollstonecraft's book has helped me, Miss Smith. There is a way I can get on with my life after all, for I would hope I am not about to be abandoned or become penniless like the heroine in the story. Perhaps I can become more like you and help in your clinic. You could teach me the rudiments of herbal medicines and I could feel useful again.'

'All those things are possible, Miss Staines, but not probable. Your family is wealthy and of good standing and I know for a fact that your brother would do anything in his power to see you happy.'

'But I cannot move in the circles I once did. Society will turn its back on me when they know.'

'Then turn your back upon them first. Lives can be lived with passion and joy in places away from the *ton*. You can certainly help in my clinic after the baby arrives, but for now with your compromised health you will need to be taken care of. Your brother can do that and will. It might be hard for you to tell him and even harder for him to hear, but he is a good man and a strong one. I know that he will want you to be in the best place you can be and I think you know this, too. Deep down.'

The small nod heartened her. 'But not yet. Not quite yet.'

'Very well.'

'You will come back to see me?'

Belle made herself smile. 'I promise it. Until you no longer need me at all.'

A small thin hand closed around her own and they sat in silence, the sunlight slanting through the curtains until Lucy fell asleep. With care Belle untangled her fingers and stood. Lady Lucy was so young and trusting. A woman in Whitechapel would never have fallen for the drivel that Lucy had told her of nor would she have been lured into a quiet building and allowed him everything.

Once was enough to become pregnant. Every young girl of her acquaintance knew this as gospel.

The unfairness of life wrung deep. Was this what had happened to her all those years before? Had she been the product of such a union? A child without the strong ties of family that Lucy could at least lay claim to? A child of indifference and mistake? A child to be thrown away like rubbish? And then forgotten? For ever.

Oh, granted, she had loved Tante Alicia, but she had missed having a parent, one who might have played with her and laughed at all the things she'd seen young mothers and their children be amused by. She had seldom mingled with other children, never been taken to the places where they were. At first she had been ill, Alicia had said, and she did remember that. Then she had been confused. Her world had changed in a way she could not quite fathom and the memories of before had faded. Now it was just the ghosts of houses and the speech of people from long ago that remained.

She'd walked through life without being truly connected. That thought made her sit up, her heart beating louder, the truth of it disconcerting. But why should she think this now when last week she had been perfectly content doling out remedies and making potions?

It was because of the Earl of Thornton. He made her want things she would never have, things like permanence and a safe haven. He made her imagine that there could be another life just waiting around the corner. A life she would have had if…

My God, she was going crazy, but suddenly an inkling of what had been once for her flourished, the visits to the Thornton town house unleashing other memories. A grand house and servants and a garden that went on for ever into the distance, its edges surrounded by water. An old lady was there, too, with a kind face and a generous body, her eyes the exact same colour of her own.

But no one could tell her of that time and so these known things had slipped back into the hidden, crouching there in hope that the light would fall upon them and reveal the truth.

A knock at Lucy's bedroom door startled her.

'The Earl would like to speak with you in the library, miss, when you are finished here.' The young servant delivered his message and waited.

'Miss Staines is asleep. I will follow you down now.'

A moment later she was being shepherded through to a room towards the back of the house, one whole wall a set of doors that led out to the greenest garden Belle had ever seen. The Earl was there, standing on the lawn, a small snatch of sunlight on his hair as he turned.

'How is my sister today?' He asked this as he strode back into the room and latched the door. Shadows fell where sunlight had been only a moment before.

'She is sleeping.'

'What do you think ails her, Miss Smith?'

There was a stillness in the words, a hesitation. Belle got the impression he had not truly wished to ask her this at all.

'It is complex, your lordship.' She struggled for time, trying to conjure up some ailment that might have fitted Lucy's symptoms and failing.

'Try to make it simple, then.'

When she looked at him she understood that he had guessed far more than Lucy might have thought he would, but in this situation her professional loyalty had to lie with her patient.

'I think she needs time and tenderness. I think it may have been an infection that has resolved.'

A shutter crossed his golden eyes, an intensity replaced by indifference. She was sad to see it, but there was no other path for her to take. She had made a promise and she always kept her promises.

'Will you visit her again?'

'I shall, but I will not charge you, your lordship.'

This time he did not argue, but rang a bell that was on his desk and waited for the servant to come.

'Could you see that Miss Smith finds her way out, Harrison? If you need the carriage—' He stopped as she interrupted him.

'No. I am quite fine.'

'Then goodbye.'

So final. So emotionless. She was just another person supplying a service to an aristocratic family who must have countless need of things each and every week.

'Oh, and, Miss Smith...?'

She turned.

'Here is your book. Lucy said that she has finished with it.'

Belle stepped up to take it, making certain not to touch him inadvertently, and then she walked out.

Chapter Five

Damn. Damn. Damn. She had lied to him about his sister, for he understood that she knew far more than she let on. God, even he could now see that Lucy was with child and for a woman used to the various symptoms of a physical body such a knowledge must be staring Miss Smith right in the face.

When might others know of it? How many weeks did he have to find his sister a husband and make certain that she was safe? Had Lucy talked to Annabelle Smith and related the truth of how it had happened? That was another worry, the concern softening as he thought of her keeping Lucy's confidence when he had asked his questions.

She would not gossip. He knew that of her instinctively and was relieved. But she would lie to him, without a blink, bald lies that covered other mistruths. Her voice. Her past. Her fear of carriages and her confession that she thought herself plain. What was it she had said to him in her drunken state?

'Belle. You can call me that. Everyone else does. It means beautiful in French, but I do not think she should have named me such for I am not.'

Did she believe that, truly? And who was the 'she' who had named her, for this was not said in the way one might speak of a parent? Another person entirely, then?

He wanted to call her back and ask. He wanted to walk with her to the carriage and have one last ride in the manner of friends. More than friends? But he could not. He knew she would never flourish in society, a woman with no ties at all to the complex and convoluted world of the *ton*. It would be unfeasible and wrong to hope for it.

He should have kept the book with its fragile blue ribbons and its ridiculous ideas. No, not ridiculous, he corrected himself, but difficult. It would be a long time before the inequality that Mary Wollstonecraft spoke of between women and men was righted and these were concepts that Lucy in her brittle state of mind and body did not need to grapple with.

The day fell down upon him, a darkness settling. Annabelle Smith was gone from him with her mistruths and her lies.

The Earl of Dromorne had approached him yesterday about a union between himself and his eldest daughter. Lady Catherine was a lovely girl, a friend, but he had no inclination to follow up the proposal further. He could do a lot worse, he knew that, for she was gracious and beautiful, competent and interesting. But he could not imagine her in his bed, writhing beneath him, her face flushed with sweat and desire.

Instead he saw Miss Annabelle Smith there, her long dark hair around him and those dimples, which seldom showed, full blown upon her face. He wondered what she would taste like, feel like, smell like. They had barely touched, but each time they had there had been a shock of connection, a red-hot blaze of lust and a surprising intimacy. Her fingers upon his thighs in the drawing room, trying to wipe off hot and scalding tea, her hand beside his in the carriage, warm and small, her head against his shoulder, the breath of her tickling his neck as she lay asleep after her disastrous reaction to one and a half small glasses of white wine.

He smiled. He did not know one other person with that sort of intolerance to alcohol.

Perhaps he would instruct Shay or Aurelian to ask around about them, after all. They must have come to England quite a while ago, he deduced, given that their practice of making medicines would have taken a goodly time to establish.

Annabelle Smith and her Tante Alicia did not seem like outsiders in Whitechapel, a place that seldom took to strangers with any sense of pace or ease.

But Miss Smith held information that could ruin the reputation of the Thorntons and as such it behoved him to take precautions. If he found out things about her that were not salutary, could he use them as blackmail should she try the same with him? Would he want to? As she'd left today she had looked at him with a sense of betrayal in her sapphire-blue eyes, the light of them dimmed by comprehension. She knew she did not belong, every bit as much as he did, in the elevated world of the *ton*.

Lytton pushed a pile of work across in front of him and sat down at his desk. He was the guardian of a lot more than simply his life. He was not kind. He had already told Annabelle that when she had said he was. Business required a hardness and he was a highly successful businessman. It was just the way it was and the way it would have to be.

He opened his drawer and found her note listing all of the ways that she had spent her ten pounds. The difference between them was encapsulated in this little message. Annabelle Smith cared about everyone while he protected his family. While she saw ten pounds as a veritable fortune he could spend that in the blink of an eye. On a bottle of perfect wine or on a new pair of boots. Or simply by throwing it on to the gambling table and not really caring if he ever got it back. She'd written a thank-you note, something he doubted he'd ever do. Things came to him easily and without much effort. The horse from Huntington was one example. He could sell it at the Thursday auctions for a hundred pounds at Tattersall's or he could hold on to it to breed more colts and recover the money ten times over.

His world was bound by nothing and Miss Annabelle Smith's world was bound by everything.

He folded her note carefully and tucked it into the ornate wooden box where he kept things he did not want to lose, wondering about the connotations of such a choice even as he closed the lid.

'I think I lived somewhere else before coming to you, Tante Alicia. I saw a glimpse of a life I used to have when I was at the Thornton town house.'

Her aunt frowned heavily and shooed Stanley off her lap. When she stood Belle saw that her back must be sore again and that the knee she had hurt last summer falling over the front step was also playing up.

Part of her wanted to take back the words and

allow her aunt some rest, but the other stronger part just could not.

'I saw a woman in my mind, too. An old woman who had eyes the same colour as my own. I need to know more, Tante Alicia. I need to know what these memories mean and who these people are.'

'Sometimes it is better just to leave the past alone, Annabelle. Things happen for a reason and to drag them all up again can be futile and hurtful. The future is there before you, to be met with enthusiasm and eagerness. I should concentrate on that if I was you.'

'Hurtful? For me, you mean?'

Her mind whirled at this new small piece of information and then seized on another bit of the puzzle. 'You said I was sick when I came to you? How sick?'

'Sick enough to die had you simply been left.'

'To die of what?'

'An injury.' Alicia said this loudly, but caught herself as her voice rose further. 'Someone had hit you, hurt you on numerous occasions. These are the truths that can wound, Belle, honesties that are pointless and avoidable.'

Belle stepped back, the summer air chilling as the possibilities of what had happened to her funnelled down. 'Did the nun who brought me to you say who had wounded me?'

'She did, but…' Her aunt stopped mid-sentence, indecision written across her face.

'Who was it? I have to know.'

'Your father. He was a violent man by all the accounts of those at the inn in which they had stayed.'

'They?'

'Your mother and him. It was your mother, not a servant, who brought you to the Notre-Dame de la Nativité and implored the nuns to look after you. She had been hit herself, Sister Maria said, but she would not stay for any doctoring. It was you she wanted protected and safe.'

So much new information and so unexpected. So many facts that she hadn't had before. A picture of a family in turmoil. It was hard to take it in. No wonder her aunt had kept her silence.

'But you don't know their names?'

'I do not. I promise you.'

'Or any information as to where they went next? The mother and father?'

'None.'

'What of the innkeeper? Would he know?'

'There was a fire there the following winter. Both the innkeeper and his wife and any records they may have kept perished in it.'

A further untraceable end. Another way of finding out nothing.

'I have not told you this before, but your mother did leave a Bible with Sister Maria. There was no front-piece in it though, no signature. It was a simple clean copy like a thousand others of the same ilk.'

'Is it here still?'

'Yes.' Alicia walked across to the bookcase at the end of the room and drew out a small burgundy-covered tome, placing it into Belle's outstretched hands.

An Anglican Bible. The King James version. It felt so ordinary, but it wasn't. Her mother had touched this once, as she had handed over a broken daughter. Was it a message of hope or of religion or of scripture? Looking through it, she saw there were no turned-down pages, no special places that had been made different. When she brought it up to her face there was only the smell of ink and age. Dust was there, too, the passing time gathered in leather.

'I've looked many times myself, Annabelle, for a clue. There are none.'

But there were, Belle thought. She was Anglican and she was loved. By a mother who had tried her best to save her and then disappeared. By a woman who could not protect herself, but would ensure her daughter's well-being.

The enormity of such a discovery had her sitting. If this message of love was the only thing she ever found out about her past, it would be enough. To know she was wanted. To understand that even in violence devotion had won.

'Would Sister Maria still be alive, do you think?'

'I don't know. Perhaps?'

'Then I could send a letter to her at the church in Moret-sur-Loing?'

Alicia crossed the room to sit beside her. 'Now that you've remembered a few things, it is probable you will remember more. You are English so some members of your family might still be here.'

'Is that why we came to London?'

'No. France was in a turmoil and I thought you could be in danger if we stayed. You were still too young to be truly safe and I wanted to protect you.'

And here was another honourable guardian, a woman who would leave behind all she knew for the custody of a child who was not her own. Belle took her old aunt's hand and felt the crepe-thin skin, the sun from the fading day sending small last shards of light down upon them, dust motes swirling in the eddies.

Outside Whitechapel burst into night noises, the men coming home from the pubs, the merchandisers selling fish and bread for tea, the children running in dirty tumbling bundles home through the narrow and poverty-stricken alleys. The proper order of life had been turned upside down only for her and there was a reassurance in that as she sat clutching her mother's Bible.

Annabelle Smith came again to Portman Square the following Wednesday and Lytton was waiting for her.

'Could I have a word with you in the library, Miss Smith?'

Today she wore an old blue gown with a half-jacket in red. The hat she sported was too large for her head, the front of it falling down over her forehead in a way that looked almost comical. Why did she never look as he expected? She carried a bunch of white daisies, too, wrapped in newspaper.

'For your sister,' she explained when she saw him looking. 'They grow in one of my patients' garden and so I asked her if I could pick some.'

'I see. Could you sit down for a moment?' Already this meeting was veering off to some place he did not wish it to go and he was pleased when they reached the library and were alone.

With care she did as he asked, folding her skirts across her legs so that not even the tiniest piece of skin showed above her boots or below the hemline.

'I have reason to believe that my sister is with child, Miss Smith.'

Lytton saw the shock of it on her face, the darkening eyes, the way her tongue licked her top lip. The utter stillness that was so unlike her.

'I was hoping you might have some more details to add to what I know.'

Her answer came very quietly. 'What is it you do know?'

So she didn't deny it. The dark rush of sorrow made him swallow. 'Very little. My sister has always been secretive and as such it is now difficult to see the way forward, to ensure the child has a father and she has a place in society.'

'She will not marry him, your lordship.'

His heart thumped at this statement. Loudly.

'I told your sister that you would always be protective of her and that she was safe here with you.'

'Which, of course, she will be, but—'

She did not let him finish.

'He will not just get away with it. The man who did this to her. I promised her that, at least.'

Lytton was horrified and could not believe what he was hearing. 'It is not your problem to deal with, Miss Smith, it is mine. Who is he?' He tried to keep the fury from his tone, but failed.

'I am a healer, your lordship, and the things

a patient relates to me in confidence are for my ears alone. If your sister wishes it different, she will tell you.'

'God. I want to kill him!' There was no kindness left in him now. If she had given him a name he would have primed his guns and left Annabelle there, revenge banishing reason and eliminating sense.

'I was thinking more in the line of a rough up.' Her voice came quietly.

'A rough up?' He stood. 'With a group of assorted strong men from Whitechapel? A measured punishment that was untraceable?'

She nodded.

'No. I will not let you do that. Nothing is untraceable and when you are caught...'

'The seething shifting population of Whitechapel stays well out of the way of the law. Being caught, as you put it, is not something that happens often there. More normally the world just goes on a little different from the way it was before and the one who is at fault is punished.'

The Earl of Thornton was furious. Belle could see it on his face and in his stance and in the balled fists he held rigidly at his side. Men often struck out in anger in Whitechapel when they held the same look of violence and a new worry surfaced. Would he be like that?

Rising from her chair, she took a step back, bringing her reticule between them. If it was even possible, his eyes blackened further, one hand reaching out to take her arm.

'I would not hurt you. Ever. Believe at least that of me, Miss Smith.'

She did have faith in these ground-out words, impossible as they might seem, as she tipped her head to observe him. He was so beautiful up close, his eyes webbed in a lighter gold, a masculinity that was undeniable and worrying. She wanted to lose herself in such a glance and be taken to the point of no return, all logic melted.

Kiss me.

Had she said this? Relief welled when she realised she had not. But he must have seen the echo of it on her face as she turned away, this raw thought making her shake, shock scrawled in waves across her body. She wanted him, she did, wanted him to simply reach out and take her lips with his. She wanted to kiss him in the way women had kissed men all across the centuries, without barriers or reasons or explanation.

In her whole life she had been distant with men, detached and reserved. But with Lytton Staines, the Earl of Thornton, there was an awareness that was startling, almost discomforting, a sort of sentience that held no true understanding.

Stars hide your fires;
let not light see my black and deep desires.

Shakespeare's words tumbled around and around in her head, the rhythm allowing her some equanimity. Others in history and literature had felt like her and they had managed, though Macbeth's dubious example was perhaps not quite what she was after. But the inclination to hide her feelings from both others and herself felt mildly honourable and so the words stayed. A protection to what lay beneath.

'Children are always a gift, your lordship, even ones that come unexpectedly. Your sister is young, but she is a survivor and the Thornton name can conceal much.'

She needed to bring the conversation back before she faltered, needed it to be about Lucy and her child and the future and not about the feelings that simmered between them or about the violence that hovered close.

'You truly believe this, that there is the propensity to recover from this?'

'A huge bulk of the population survives without having anything at all to do with society. Your sister can help out at the Whitechapel clinic, she can teach other younger girls how to read and write, she can...'

'Stop. You have no idea what is at stake here. With a child born out of wedlock my sister will never have a place to live safely, never be accepted by all the people she knows. Who would marry her now?'

'Maybe she is not after marriage.' Her own ire had fired. 'Maybe she wants freedom and options and other possibilities.'

'Like the pathway you have chosen?'

'A husband is not always the way to lasting happiness, your lordship.'

'God.' The huge chasm that yawned between them widened further. Annabelle Smith had no idea of the life he lived, the conventions and expectations, the unspoken truths of privilege. And how could she? How could he even have supposed it? Her voice and her body and her startling eyes had mesmerised him, made him foolish, were still making him foolish, but it needed to stop. Now.

'How much could I pay you in order for you to keep quiet about this whole...situation, Miss Smith?'

'Pardon?' She looked puzzled.

'Blackmail, Miss Smith. I want to make certain that it never happens because of this. What sum would keep you from mentioning my sister's circumstances to anyone else...for ever?'

He felt her breathe out, felt the loss of her respect with an ache. 'The sum of honour, your lordship, and if you had to ask such a question then you have none.'

He smiled, though there was a tightness in his throat. 'I have thousands of pounds to my name and a good number of them could be at your disposal if they allowed me to ascertain silence. Consider that.' Sometimes, thought Lytton, it took a few tries to get a person to reveal their true colours. How many times in the business world had he seen this? 'If you won't think of yourself, Miss Smith, then think of the difference such an amount might make in Whitechapel.'

'To sell my soul on the account of your deceit? To be devalued by standards that are repugnant to me? I think not.'

'You were the one who lied about my sister's malady.' He could not let it go, not just yet, not till he understood her purpose completely.

'I did not tell you of her condition because she asked me not to, as my patient.'

'And as the one paying the bills am I accorded no rights whatsoever? As a brother? As a guardian?'

'I cannot be the puppet of two masters, your lordship. It is neither feasible nor advisable.'

'Who are you then exactly, Miss Smith? No other soul from Whitechapel whom I have met speaks the King's English as you do and yet refuses the chance of a lucrative handout. If I asked around about your history, what might I find?'

The fear on her face made him falter.

'I do not wish to hurt you. I only wish to keep my family safe.'

'Then allow me to do my job, your lordship, and see to your sister's health needs. That is all. Afterwards I doubt we shall ever meet again.'

He nodded and summoned a servant, the relief he saw in her eyes as she left more than evident.

Perhaps she hated him, Belle thought. Perhaps it was easier. Perhaps in the full comprehension of the differences between them it would be a more sensible thing to feel. He had mistresses and a woman who had been handpicked for him in marriage by his parents. He had others, too, who were hopeful of a relationship according to his sister, for Lucy, by her own admission, had been beating off enquiries about him ever since arriving in society.

Annabelle sat down on her bed and put her head in her hands. The Earl thought she might blackmail him about his sister's pregnancy?

What sort of a person would think such a thing? One with a huge estate to run and a family who was falling to pieces all around him, that was who.

He did not trust her. Perhaps he did not trust anyone as faith diminished under responsibility. What would it be like to live with a man like that, a man who imagined everyone his enemy, adversaries around every corner.

Reaching for her Bible, she held it close, wishing her mother were here to talk with, to ask advice from, to alleviate her utter loneliness. As she did this she noticed the stitching on the bottom back corner of the leather cover had unravelled, a small piece of paper tucked away inside suddenly seen.

With care she prised it out to find a single name written there. Annalena. The blue ink was faded and the writing was cursive, an old style of handwriting that was prevalent in the borrowed books from the printer in London.

Annalena.

She had no memory of this name, try as she might to find one, as she said it out aloud to herself in as many different ways that she thought it could be pronounced.

This little clue was enthralling and captivated her attention. Was it her mother's name? The woman with the beaten face who had thrust her at the nun at the Catholic church? Was it a place, somewhere denoting her origins? Or the name of the house in the green fields descending to a lake?

Annalena? Blue eyes were there. Eyes the same colour as her own. Piercing and sad. Saying goodbye to her. Holding her close. Crying.

'Come back to me, little one. Come back when you can.'

Belle felt her own tears pouring down her face here in her room years and years later. A mother. No. That did not quite seem right. An older woman. A grandmother?

Nannalena? Another remembered word. She had called her that, there in the green fields with the manor at her back, a winding moat across the front façade hiding a small river running to the sea.

She was lost from it. Lost from this and the woman. Annalena. Lost from sight and yet remembering. Abandoned, but loved. Once. Her own name was a part of this one. Anna. The whisper of history reached out and she heard them calling her, among the green of trees and flowers.

'Anna. Anna. Where are you?'

'Here,' she whispered. 'I am lost and waiting.'

How could she find them again, these people, with such a small and tiny clue? She could not ask for help from her aunt and she did not have the funds to leave London and search the rural countryside for a needle in a haystack.

She needed to remember more, but try as she might she could not. A headache was all she got for her trouble. That and a blinding realisation that she would need to be patient.

The Earl of Thornton's words today also reverberated around in her head.

'Who are you then exactly, Miss Smith? No other soul from Whitechapel whom I have met speaks the King's English...'

Her secrets were beginning to hunt her out, the small enclave she had lived in here widening with her recent visits to Portman Square.

There were answers close and possibilities which both frightened and excited her.

'Who are you, Miss Smith?'

It felt it would not be too much longer before she found her answers.

Chapter Six

Two days later she was back again at Portman Square and Lady Lucy looked so much better. It was youth, Belle supposed, for at twenty the body could bounce back from things that a decade later might only be managed with much more difficulty. The Earl of Thornton's sister made her feel old and after the interview with Lord Thornton in the library the other day she was already on guard, a melancholy assailing her that was unlike anything she'd ever known before. She hoped she would not see him almost as much as she hoped she would.

He was lost to her, the Earl. She could see it in his eyes and hear it in his voice. The end of regard. The beginning of distance. His sister, however, was more than animated.

'I am so glad you have come, Miss Smith, for

I have begun to take note of Mrs Wollstonecraft's words and such strength has been a considerable help. I feel now as though I can go on
with my life in a renewed way.'

'And the child?'

'I shall retire to Balmain and live in the country with my mother until I decide what must be
done next. London feels lessened for me now
and exhausting and I need to recover.'

'Your brother knows you are with child. He
has asked me for the name of the father.'

Lucy nodded her head. 'I thought he knew,
for I could see it in his eyes when he spoke
to me yesterday. If I tell him it was Huntington, I think he will kill him and then what will
happen? The estate has only just recovered
from my father's unwise excess and if Thorn
is thrown into gaol for his act of revenge then
where will it leave us all? My brother is a man
who likes to be on top of things, you see, and
one who dislikes any surprise. I think you are
a great surprise to him, Miss Smith.'

Now this was new. 'How do you mean, Miss
Staines?'

'Lucy. I wish you to call me that. Thorn is

a man who is in control of every part of the Earldom. The finance, the family, the estates. My sister, brother and I have probably all in our own ways been trials to him, but he has handled everything with aplomb. With you he has been knocked askew, for I think he cannot believe that a woman might choose her way in life without a man and enjoy it.'

Annabelle was astonished. In little more than a week the younger sister of the Earl of Thornton seemed to have grown up and blossomed. She was no longer downtrodden or sad and, although she was still very thin, she also looked healthy.

'I also want to ask something of you, Miss Smith, something personal.'

Annabelle nodded.

'I have decided to let go of my anger and, although I might have intimated to you that revenge was something I was after, I no longer feel that way at all. I want now to simply enjoy my baby without being held back by anything.'

'A wise choice, I think.'

'So the favour that I would ask of you is to forget all I told you and be happy for me.'

'I shall do that, Lucy. My aunt would applaud your choice, for there are things in my family that have been difficult and she is one who would look to the future with hope rather than to past regrets.'

'I knew you would understand. I hope you might be persuaded to visit me at Balmain. I could send the carriage down if you would deign to come. Perhaps when the baby is near time for I would feel far happier and safer if you were there.'

'I should like that.'

'I also want to give you something, Miss Smith. Something to remember me by.'

She walked across to a desk at one side of the room and extracted a small parcel wrapped in coloured paper and red ribbon.

'It is only a small token, I know, but it reminds me so much of you.'

When Annabelle opened it she saw it was a painting of flowers done in oil.

'It's a painting I bought last year in the Academy's Summer Exhibition. The fallen bloom is me and you, Miss Smith, are represented in the strength of the roses above.'

'It's beautiful.' And it was. How could have Lucy known she enjoyed images of flowers? Perhaps her brother had told her of the paintings in the front room at White Street. Her own attempts at mimicking nature seemed naive against the detail of this image.

'I shall hang it on my wall, Lucy, and think of you. I am sorry I have nothing to give in return...'

'Save courage, I think, and fortitude, things for a while I was badly lacking. I bought another copy of Mrs Wollstonecraft's book after my brother said he had returned the one you leant to me, just to keep. You were clever to think that it might be helpful.'

'You are not the first young woman to need advice, Lucy, and you certainly will not be the last.'

'See, that is what I mean, Miss Smith. Whenever you give advice it is with sense and vigour. I will miss you.'

'I will miss you, too, but if you talk with your brother you'll understand that he loves you with all his heart and that you are lucky to have such a protector.'

Lucy nodded. 'Most people are frightened of Thorn. His success scares them off, but he is also dangerous in a precise and measured way. He does not waste emotion, I suppose, or squander sentiment. He protects his family with all that he has and he does that well.' Small fingers threaded around a lace handkerchief as she spoke, her nails still short and bitten.

The family. All the expectations of great wealth and history heaped on one man. It was no wonder the Earl of Thornton was sometimes taciturn. But he could be funny, too, and sweet. She remembered waking up in the carriage after her disastrous episode with the wine, her head having creased his linen shirt. She liked talking with him. She liked the sense of possibility edged with a danger that was fascinating. He was not a man who would bore her.

But she also knew her time with the Thorntons was coming to an end and that was as it should be. Lady Lucy would return to the country estate of Balmain and she would get on with her work in the poorer parts of London town, a few hundred miles away geographically, but a million miles apart in any other way that counted.

She clutched her beautiful oil painting and bade the Earl of Thornton's sister goodbye.

Lytton wondered what he was doing here. The Barretts' ball was well appointed, well attended and well thought of, but he was troubled.

Lady Catherine Dromorne stood with him, every piece of her in perfect place as she related to him details of the newest scandal of the *ton*. Not in a mean way, but in the way of a woman who could not countenance any behaviour that veered away from the narrow expectations of society, expectations she had been brought up with from the very cradle.

He felt restless and on edge. It had been three weeks since he had last seen Miss Annabelle Smith. She had left the house without a glance back, his sister's renewed health allowing no other necessary appointment in the future. Oh, granted, vague plans had been put in place to keep in touch, but her smile had been distant and forced.

She had been glad to get away from them all, that much was plain.

Lady Catherine's voice broke into his reveries. 'I can't understand how Lord Macmillan could have imagined he would not have been seen with Mrs Julia Chambers at that time of the day in a busy street. As my father said, the end of the world as we know it is coming sooner than we think if people insist upon liaisons with such unsuitable others.'

When had Catherine begun to parrot her father? he wondered. Lytton had never noticed this trait before. His mind returned to Annabelle Smith. Was it her circumstances that had softened his own attitude to those around him, allowing the person they were to triumph over the one everybody else thought them?

Mrs Julia Chambers had been married to a man who was a bully and a cheat, his wealth never quite hiding the lowly lineage he had been raised from. He had seen Gregory Macmillan with the beauteous widow on a number of occasions lately and never thought much of it, for she always appeared well mannered and demure. He held no idea of the circumstances of her background, but, from Catherine's words of warning, presumed that she certainly did.

The same ennui that had been building now for weeks suddenly assailed him. He felt jaded and tired, the weary task of pulling the Earldom from shambles suddenly heavy. He wanted to disappear, away from society, away from expectations, away from the constant badgering of those whose own straits were needing regeneration as much as his own. Even the canning factory tonight held no joy for him, the constant demands arising from it part of the reason he felt so damned tired.

The wreck of eighteen months of hard work, the sadness over the dreadful loss of his father, his sister's ruin and Annabelle Smith's lies fed into his defeat.

He wanted more. Aurelian and Violet de la Tomber danced together in the middle of the floor and the gaze they bestowed upon each other was beguiling. He imagined them going home after this to their town house and falling into a large soft bed full of promise. It would be a happy night.

He would sleep by himself.

Weeks ago after the Susan Castleton fiasco that realisation would have been exactly what he did want, but tonight all it felt was lonely.

'You are quiet, Thornton?' Catherine's voice was husky, one of the things he had liked about her right from the start.

'Tired, I think.' He tried to rally and asked her to dance even though it was the last thing that he wished to do. Once on the floor she gazed at him directly and his heart sank when he knew it was a waltz.

'I am sorry about my father's unexpected visit a few weeks ago. He took it on himself to organise my life and come to see you. Marriage is such an enormous step, do you not think?'

She said this in a way that made it sound completely the opposite and all of Lytton's defences were instantly raised.

'We know each other too well,' he countered, recognising that this was exactly the wrong thing to have said as soon as he had uttered it.

'And you think that a negative?' She watched him so closely that he changed tack.

'The Thornton estate is consuming my time, Catherine, and I cannot see it changing much for at least a year.' He saw her shaking her head and knew what she might say next, how she might try to cajole him into another option or of how she would be happy to wait. 'I will be in the Americas on business for a few months as well. Edward Tully is going over as my representative and will need a hand. I have promised him one.'

'I have heard differently. It is whispered by solid sources that you are after a bride.'

He swore under his breath as he almost lost his step. Who the hell had told her that? He'd made it very clear to her father that he was not interested in marriage and he knew instinctively that Edward, Aurelian or Shay would not have said anything of his ridiculous outburst about marrying the first girl he saw. Had someone else overheard it?

'Right now business keeps me frantic and so does the family.'

He was relieved when the music came to a stop and he was able to escort Catherine Dromorne back to her friends and make his own way to find a drink.

Aurelian waylaid him as he went.

'You look harried, Thorn. Is Catherine Dromorne still after your hand in Holy Matrimony?'
There was humour in his tone.

'Her and half-a-dozen others. I shouldn't have
come tonight, for I am not in the mood for flir-
tation and innuendo and definitely not for marriage.'

'Lady Thomasina Dutton was asking after
you before. She has never seemed to me to be
a girl who was vapid.'

Lytton drew his hand through his hair and
swiped it back from his face. He had been smitten by Thomasina Dutton some while ago, but
tonight even her beautiful face and endearing personality were undesirable. None of the
women here appealed to him, none made his
heart beat faster or his mind imagine things
that were far more intimate.

He shut off the thoughts that lingered on a
face with dimples and sapphire-blue eyes. *Not
for me. Not ever for me.*

If he did not marry, then his younger brother's children could take over the title.

For a moment he felt displaced and dizzy, the
room swirling around him in colour and move-

ment and himself in the middle of it all, still and foreign and lost.

'Let's have a drink.' Lian's words came crashing into the silence and brought him back and he was grateful to be able to follow him to stand in the outside air on a balcony to one end of the room.

'What the hell is wrong with you, Thorn? You looked like you might fall over back there. Is the sickness Lucy has been afflicted with contagious?'

That question at least made him smile.

'No, and she is recovering daily.'

'The healer from Whitechapel did her job, then?'

'Seems to have.'

'Where is she now? Do you still see her?'

'Why should I? She was Lucy's physician, not mine.'

'A sore point, then? A raw nerve? Shay said he was much taken with the woman though she had no stomach for the drink. He said you took her home to Whitechapel by way of Hyde Park and spent three hours getting her there?'

'What are you saying, Lian?'

'The things that you are not, Thorn. I saw her this morning, by the way, in Regent Street, carrying a hefty basket. Lord Huntington was walking past and he looked most taken by her appearance. You might have competition, though he is the last man Miss Annabelle Smith needs to know at all. Remember him from school? He was a bully and a cheat.'

'He gave Edward a bloody nose the first time he met him and dragged all of us behind the sheds at one point or another. His uncle was some sort of boxing expert, if I remember rightly, and had taught him well.'

'Thank God we are no longer schoolboys.' Lian smiled and turned to look over the garden and the lights that had been placed on the small pathway.

'You looked happy tonight on the dance floor, Lian. Being married suits you. It suits Shay as well.'

'It does. It's like finding a pot of gold at the end of the rainbow. Gold I was becoming less and less sure I'd find, I might add.'

'In what way?'

'I'd given up on thinking true love could ever

be mine, but it can arrive on the single beat of the heart or an unexpected shaft of light and it can be unsettling.'

'You speak as if you think I should know this?'

'Catherine Dromorne looks like a rainbow tonight.'

'But she is not mine.'

'Then find your truth, Thorn, without compromise. Only you can know what is within here.'

His hand touched his chest, a small gesture with a large honesty attached to it.

Lytton finished his drink, refusing the next one from a passing footman.

'My life at the moment is busy, Lian. I haven't got time for further complications of the heart.

His friend's laughter was not comforting and he was about to say something when Edward Tully came out of the crowd, carrying a note.

'It's for you, Thorn. It's just been delivered.'

'Hell.' He could only think of one reason why a message would come to him here in the middle of the night and in the middle of the ball.

Lucy had returned from Balmain two days ago to stay in the city for a week and she had not been feeling well.

Clutching the missive, he gave his leave to both Lian and Edward and made for the door.

Annabelle Smith had come in the carriage he had sent to Whitechapel arriving on the town-house doorstep after one in the morning, her hair bundled at her neck and her cheeks rosy from sleep. Her aunt accompanied her.

She barely gave him notice as she asked after his sister.

'How long has she been ill?'

'Since this morning. She had stomach cramps and felt unwell.'

'Why did you not call for me earlier?'

'Lucy was sure it was only something she had eaten. She did not want a fuss.'

'Well, she is about to get one now, your lord-ship.' There was a sort of fear in her eyes, a worry that immediately transferred itself to him.

'We will see her alone if you would like to wait. This is women's business.'

'Certainly.' He was almost glad for it.

Annabelle Smith tried to reassure him as he sat on the small sofa in the parlour attached to the bedchamber. 'It will be as it will be. No amount of worry will make it different. The child is in God's hands now.'

'But your own competence must count for something, surely.'

'It does, but it is early on in the pregnancy and sometimes a baby is simply not viable. I have seen this many times before.'

He was unsure how much a statement like that helped, but attempted to dredge up the rudiments of belief. 'Thank you.'

She simply looked at him then, a stillness settling between them.

'Should I call others as well, Miss Smith? The family physician?'

'No. We are enough and also we are very... discreet.'

He swallowed. He knew that was why he had called her, Miss Annabelle Smith with her healing skills and her independence. There would be no gossip after this, whatever happened.

The chatter could be contained, isolated, and the reputation of his sister could be saved. Unless she died. That thought hit him hard and he stood even as Miss Smith and her aunt left him, the bag they carried between them large and full.

Perhaps it was a punishment, this, a penalty against a family whose patriarch had simply shot himself after gambling away the Thornton country estate. A retribution that came at a price: the price of the life of a bastard child and his mother.

He sat down again suddenly and weighed up the balance sheets. If he had been less honest, he might have kneeled to pray, but he was sure an omnipotent God would only see the falseness in such an action. It had been years since he'd truly believed in anything save the pursuit of money and to start beseeching a deity in a final hour of need seemed an empty hope and disingenuous to boot.

But he did whisper something under his breath. 'Please.' Whether it was directed at Miss Belle Smith or to the celestial power above he could not quite at that point fathom.

* * *

The clock struck five and Belle looked around the library, surprised by the time and its passing. Her aunt had been taken home in the Thornton carriage and Lucy was sleeping, tucked upstairs gently in a bed that was warm and safe and hers.

'There was no chance?' The Earl asked this from the seat opposite in his downstairs library.

'None. I tried.'

'I know.'

Silence resumed.

'Will my sister recover?'

'She will recover as well as any woman can after the loss of a child, no matter what its history.'

'Of course.'

He'd had lemonade brought up from the kitchens and slices of fruit bread. She was grateful for it.

It was almost companionable here, in the very early morning before the house began to move, books all around them and a muted dawn on the grass outside. Time between time. She often felt like this after the death of a patient, only a thin line separating the quick from the dead.

'No matter how much you think you know, it can never be enough to save them all.' The words slipped out, unbidden.

'But you tried and that is the difference.'

'One day, years and years on, there will be ways found to save them, these very little ones.'

She saw the leap of surprise in his eyes and she wondered why she might have told him this. Goodness, the Thorntons had thought her a witch when first she had come here and proclamations like this probably did her cause little good. But she needed to talk, too, needed to assuage the loss and find acceptance, the grief raw in her words.

'It's the young patients that stay with you, I think. The promise of what might have been and now will never be. The loss of all those years.'

She tried to keep the utter desolation from her voice, but failed.

'At least your work is honourable,' he said finally. 'At least you try to fashion a better world, a happier one, and if you can't then what is left is still enhanced because of your caring.'

She liked his explanation and smiled. 'I

sometimes think that it takes pieces of me, little pieces that I can't recover. Tante Alicia says she deliberately does not let this happen, but I... I do not seem to be able to help it.'

Sipping on her lemonade, she looked at him directly. This morning she couldn't be bothered hiding from him, she needed to say what she said and he was the person here to listen. An earl or not, he was still a brother. A brother who had lost something as well.

He sat forward, his legs long and folded. His boots were of a shiny black leather and his buckles were silver, the metal embossed with a coat of arms. Small details that would for ever stick with her.

'My job takes pieces from me, too, and it is nowhere near as honourable. To save a life, even to try to save one seems to me to be unparalleled.'

The light had changed now, creeping in a more distinct form across the perimeter of the garden, changing shadows.

'If you would like to stay here at the town house, a room can be readied?'

'No. Thank you.'

'Then I almost hesitate to mention payment for tonight's services, for what price does one place upon a life?'

'I did not save one.'

'But Lucy is safe. You made sure of that.'

The tears that she had held back all night suddenly began to fall and she swiped at them angrily, not wishing to give into the sorrow.

He did not move forward and for that she was grateful. Right then she did not need the physical.

'I cried for my father.' His words. A shared confession. She was certain he had told nobody else in all the world such a thing.

She looked up and into his soul, bared there before her.

'I hated him for doing it, for killing himself in the bed of a mistress after gambling away the family estate. How could that be tempered? How could I fix it?'

'The ruin of a family name? Like tonight? Again?'

'Exactly.' The word was harsh and sad. 'I am an earl, Miss Smith, a guardian of history and a minder of time and place, and while my sister's child would have caused a ruction in the fabric of the Thorntons, I still did not wish it away.'

'Then I am glad for it.'

'Just as I am glad you were here, too.'

She nodded and breathed out. Perhaps this was all that she had needed, a heartfelt thanks that encompassed his own secrets. A new beginning on an equal footing.

She was so tired she could barely move and she did not want to. There was something infinitely satisfying about sitting with a man who was strong enough to show his vulnerability after she had shown him hers. He did not seem to be in any hurry either as he leant back and watched her. The gleam in his eyes was brighter now.

'Your reputation is growing by the day, Miss Smith. I have had many enquiries about your services.'

'It is unusual for me to venture past Whitechapel, my lord. Generally, I feel happier there.'

'How long have you lived in White Street?'

'Almost twenty years now. Where does that time go? You look up and next thing years have past.'

'Why were you there? In France?'

'My parents were travellers.'

'They did not return home? Your mother and father?'

She shook her head. 'They died.'

She gave him the words like a truth even though she knew it was not one. But the alternative was too hard to say. *I was abandoned there. I was beaten up and left. Sick to death in a church.*

Now she was lying and the Miss Annabelle Smith he was more familiar with was back. Prickly. Independent. Unusual.

He did not want to ask her anything else because more falsehoods would wreck what was left of this one rare night and he liked that he had a memory of her that was honest and that the awkwardness of the other day seemed lessened.

'Will you return to see to my sister?'

'Yes. Tomorrow I shall come again, my lord. Sleep is what she needs now as well as good food and kind company.'

'Then I shall make sure that she receives both.'

She used his title at such random moments. Sometimes he thought she might have almost forgotten the distance in status between them. Sometimes he did, too.

His formal attire was so different from the clothes Annabelle had pulled on in the middle of the night and the fine bones in her face were drawn over sorrow, the flames of candles highlighting the startling blue in her eyes reddened with fatigue.

He would have liked to ask after the child that was gone but he didn't, reasoning that it would have been very small and she probably did not want such a reminder anyway. Her fingers were red, blisters running down the inside length of her forefinger, and when she noticed him looking she hurried in to explain.

'The hotter the water the better the outcome.'

He smiled at that. Such a concise and abridged medical statement with no pretence in any of it. He wished he could have leant over and taken her hand into his own, soothing pain, finding touch. But she gave no impression of wanting this, unlike all the women who had flirted outrageously with him in the Barrett's ballroom.

Two worlds separated distinctly.

Belle felt the connection between them, a sort of shared sorrow and common tie. The Earl was by far the most handsome man she had ever laid her eyes upon and yet it was not his appearance that riveted her. It was the pain in his eyes and the care he held for his sister. It was the sharing of his own fears and his unexpected openness.

His father's death had shocked her and yet he had told it to her without amendment. Why? Did he mean to frighten her off? Or was he trying to draw closer?

She knew nothing more of him other than what she had discovered in the half-dozen times they had met. She knew he was not married, but was there a woman with whom he had an understanding. His mother and sister had spoken of a mistress, but Belle guessed that was par for the course for the very wealthy. They did not give their hearts easily and when they did it was with a proviso. She had heard the stories after all many times around the fireplaces off the Whitechapel Road. The excesses of the very rich made them careless of feelings, it was said, and faithless. This certainly appeared to be the case with the Earl's father.

Thornton smelt of perfume and of women. His clothes tonight were nothing like she had seen him in before. They were dark, formal and well cut, the fabrics soft. He looked tired, too, his hair brushed back off his face in a quick sleight of hand, the colour of toffee and cinnamon and mid-brown autumn leaves.

Lucy had seemed more indifferent to the miscarriage of her child than he was. She had been quiet for nearly all of the doctoring until the very end when she had asked whether it was a boy or a girl.

'It is hard to tell this early.' Belle had said the words with kindness, but Lucy had simply turned away in her bed towards the wall and refused further conversation.

Perhaps it was for the best, this miscarriage, Annabelle thought. Perhaps there were things that in the elevated world of the *ton* were impossible to recover from.

She thought of all the young women in White-chapel whose births she had attended. Many of these were products of violence or rape and yet the babies had been taken in and loved.

More differences. Further disparities.

With care she stood then, holding her bag before her and watching the Earl of Thornton rise, too.

'I should go for it is late.'

'Or early depending how one looks at it.' Already the birds were waking outside.

'Someone should stay with your sister at all times for this day at least. It is just a precaution. If she begins to bleed again, call for me immediately.'

'I shall see that is done, Miss Smith, and thank you, for everything.'

He looked as if he might lean forward and take her hand. Indeed, she got the distinct impression that he started to before checking himself. The clock in the corner struck five thirty, a hollow sound in the oncoming dawn.

Chapter Seven

Her aunt was up when she arrived home.

'You stayed awake, Tante, and it is so very late?'

'I could not sleep. There is a difference. Who is the Earl of Thornton to you, Belle?'

'He is the brother of my patient. He is the one who has been paying the bills.'

'I think he is dangerous. I think you should stay well away from him, with his fine house and expensive clothes and eyes that look you over from top to bottom.'

For a second Annabelle was dumbfounded. 'You have it wrong, Tante Alicia. I doubt he even sees me for who I am. It's the way of those folk, don't you see?'

'No. He is a man who is used to getting exactly what he wants and right now that is you.

And as soon as it is difficult, which it would be given the differences between you, he will throw you over for the woman he should have been courting, the Countess he ought to have married, the one his family likes and who society welcomes.'

'My God.' Belle suddenly understood exactly what her aunt was saying. 'It happened to you, didn't it? In France when you were young? Someone just like the Earl?'

The fury in those dark eyes told her the truth even as Alicia tried to shake it away.

'It's why you did not marry? Why you had no children? Did you love him?'

But Alicia had gone back to her room, the door shutting hard. Death, betrayal and love. The day was full of pain and Belle knew there would be no simple remedy. With a sigh she dropped her bag on the floor before lying down fully dressed on the bed. The last thing she remembered before sleep came was the Earl of Thornton on the steps of his town house, watching her leave. Large and still and alone.

* * *

Dromorne arrived again the following afternoon at Portman Square and this time he was not to be fobbed off so easily for Catherine accompanied him.

'You have given the impression that you were more than interested in my daughter, Thornton, and because of it other suitors have held back on asking for permission to get to know her better. She is almost twenty-two now and three Seasons in your company have meant she is dangerously near to being left on the shelf. I need an agreement, Thornton, and I need it soon.'

Part of him just wanted to turf Lord Dromorne out on his ear, but the man was old and had been a family friend for many years. Besides that, he did not look particularly well, his face flushed red and bloated and his pulse racing. Catherine, next to Dromorne, looked so miserable she could barely meet his eyes.

'Say what you need to, Daughter, and do not hold back.'

Her brown eyes were full of embarrassment. 'I thought... I thought that we were...promised, my lord. I have not looked at another and I am old now.'

'Twenty-two is hardly old.' God, compared to his years it seemed damn young. The trap of it all blurred his future even as fire sprang into her words.

'It is when you are a female. It is as old as you can possibly be until you can no longer expect to find a suitable marriage. Everyone says so.'

This was far worse than he had thought. He had imagined Catherine being as rebellious as he was when he knew she was coming with her father to see him. He thought this whole mess would be sorted without fuss in a few moments, but he had miscalculated badly. His own words from a few months back were also a part of this mix up. He had intimated to his friends he would marry the next passably good-looking woman who could bear children. Well, here was one before him who was more than beautiful and who now professed to be ruined in making a fine marriage and all because of him. If he did not offer something Lord Drom-orne would be sure to spread the gossip of the reckless Thorntons and all the memories of his father's stupidity would be back as the main topic of scandal yet again. None of this would be helpful to his newly expanding but fledgling businesses.

Annabelle Smith's face came to mind, but he knew deep down that anything between them would be hopeless. They would both ruin each other. Still, he could not quite let it go.

'Give me twelve weeks, Catherine. If by then you have not found another whom you feel you might make a life with, then I will court you. I promise it. We have always been friends, but I had not imagined anything more. I am sorry.'

The frown on her forehead deepened, but her father looked happier. 'I will take your word as the unbreakable troth of a gentleman, Thornton.'

'You do that.' His words were angry and harsh and had Catherine not been standing there with her head bent and her hands working the material around and around in her fetching pink skirt he would have said more.

At best he could try to talk with her alone and reason with her. At worst he would be attached in twelve weeks to a woman of good birth whom his family liked and who would make an admirable countess.

The tangle of it all stuck in his throat.

Lytton visited Shay an hour later, pleased to see his friend at home and alone. In the library a few moments later and with a drink in hand he felt able to confess the exact reason as to why he had come. 'Dromorne came to see me today.' The words came quietly and Shay looked up.

'What about?'

'He thinks I have misled his daughter into an expectation of marriage for these past three years. He has now come with the express intention of collecting his debt.'

'What did you say?'

'What could I say?'

'Surely you did not consent?'

'I hedged. I told him that in twelve weeks if Catherine still had not found a man she loved, then I would court her properly. She was there so I could hardly say different.'

'I see.'

'Do you? I am thirty-five years old. I need an heir. I need a countess who can cope with all that the position entails. I need stability for my family, for Lucy and Prudence and David. And for Mama. I am the head of a family that is fragile and the only way to save it might be to sacrifice myself.'

'The speech of a martyr. *"Under love's heavy burden do I sink."* God. Leave England if you must on the pretence of business, but do not marry a woman whom you could never truly love.'

'It is not so black and white, Shay. I have a friendship with Catherine and I do respect her, but honour is all I have left at the end of the day and I can't just abandon that. My father did and I have hated him for it every day, ever since.'

'Your father was an ass, but you were always a good man, Thorn, under the wildness, so here's to you and happiness and a heartfelt warning that a whole life is a long time to live in the shadow of regret.'

Shay brought up his glass and Lytton smiled. 'I'll drink to that.'

Whitechapel Road was a long one and today a group of sheep and cattle were being driven through to the slaughterhouse a few streets away. Caught behind people and animals, Belle gazed around at the noise and the movement, a canvas of commerce and poverty and just plain hard living. Sometimes she loved this place, even despite its obvious problems. It was vital and busy and ever changing, the sedate and beautiful square of the Earl of Thornton's a far cry from here.

Here anything was possible, if not probable, and the folk who inhabited the lodgings were as diverse as the houses themselves. The milkmaids with their balance of buckets and their beautiful skin, the fish vendors, the children with their dirty faces and bare feet, the loose women, the clergy, the constabulary, the drunks. It was a tapestry of colour, form and shape, against a backdrop of violence and community.

Belle had walked these streets since she was twelve and newly come from France. She knew the alleyways to avoid and the taverns that harboured the worst of the thieves and felons. She understood the safety of daytime and the dangers of the night. There were so many faces here that were familiar now.

It was not often a stranger could traverse these streets without notice, but she was sure one had for she'd the uncanny feeling that someone had been following her for a few days now. Someone who did not belong here, someone who was an outsider. Someone who was watching her.

She had turned often and quickly, but had never caught the perpetrator save for once on the very end of Whitechapel Road near Aldgate when a man at a distance dressed in the clothes of a gentleman had observed her and made to follow.

She had lost him easily, turning into Goulstone Street and then Wentworth, her increasingly fast flight putting an end to any continued surveillance. She had said nothing to Tante Alicia nor to Rose, not wanting to worry them with accusations that could be pointless, after all.

Who would follow her? Most people here were pleased for her expertise in medicines and ailments and would knock at her door if they had need of help. Everybody knew that she was as poor as they were. She did not pick or choose patients, but treated each one cross-ing the threshold of her lodging with the same courtesy as she had the one before. A fair and equal doctoring. She was therefore left alone to do as she willed in the parish and there had never once in all the years since arriving been an incident that had made her question the safety of walking here.

Until now.

She breathed a sigh of relief as she saw Rose-mary crossing the street towards her.

'I heard you went back to the Earl of Thorn-ton's house the day before yesterday in Port-man Square, Belle?'

'I did. I was there briefly this morning, too. Miss Staines had sickened and needed medi-cines.'

Annabelle hated lying to her friend, but she could understand the Earl's point in respect-ing confidentiality. He had not been there this morning, but his sister had looked a lot brighter and was talking of going to the family estate in the country to recuperate. Perhaps she was relieved to have lost the child and to have a future that was largely untarnished before her once again. Belle had not mentioned the baby at all for the girl did not seem to encourage it, merely checking her stomach and pulse and temperature.

There was an awkwardness between them now, though. The end of one relationship and the beginning of another. Perhaps if she had been in Lady Lucy's shoes she might have felt the same, a reminder of an episode so terrible she wanted no more to recall it.

Belle had left quickly, knowing that she might not be back again and knowing, too, that the young woman was on the road to a good recovery.

'Was the Earl present?' Rose looked more than interested as she asked this.

'He was not.'

'I liked him. I thought he was beautiful.'

Belle laughed. 'You barely met him.'

'But I can always tell if people's souls are good ones. It's my strength. His was pure.'

'I doubt if even he would tell you that was so, had you asked.'

'He's spoken of his character? With you? My goodness, tell me all about it.'

'Rose, stop. I will probably never see him again and that is just as it should be. People pass in and out of my life all the time, their need great until it is not.'

They were coming to the main road now on the edge of Whitechapel, the thoroughfare widening out. Belle had promised Tante Alicia that she would visit the markets for herbs as their supplies were running low and Rose was going the same way. She was glad for the company as they stood on the side of the road, ready to cross together.

The carriage came from nowhere, skidding in the wet towards them and throwing them both to the ground. Belle felt her head whack against stone and knew a sharp pain in her right wrist where she had tried to shield her fall. Rosemary beneath her was lying very still.

Panic banished a lethargy that was becoming more appealing.

'Rose. Rose. Are you all right?'

Her friend's eyes fluttered. 'I think so. What happened?'

'A carriage hit us and it did not stop.' Already she could see the back of it turning a corner further off, nothing from this distance to distinguish it from the others that plied the road. She felt sick and shaking and, recognising shock, placed her hand at her neck to count her pulse. Fast and thready. Swallowing, she tried to take stock of her fright, but the tunnel about her was darkening and then the world was simply falling away.

She woke a few moments later propped up against a brick door well with many people about her. There was something tight around her head and she put her hand up to see what it was.

'Leave it there, Miss Smith, it's a bandage.' The man who brought them coal was kneeling before her, his brow furrowed. 'Your head was bleeding badly and the flow needed to be stopped.'

Rose was beside her now, her face white. 'You fainted, Belle. How do you feel?'

'Better. I am sure I will be fine.' She tried to come to her haunches, but the world swam dizzily and so she sat back. 'Give me ten minutes and we will start for home. Did you see the carriage who hit us, Mr Curtis?'

'Not really. It were a fine one, though, and the driver were in livery.'

That was new. And worrying.

Mrs Roberts from a few streets away had also come forward. 'Gracious me, Miss Smith, you were lucky you were not both killed. My son Harold is here with me as he is home for a few hours to see us. I will get him to help you.'

Belle wanted to say no because Mrs Roberts's son was a kitchen worker in a fine house in Portman Square. The woman had told her of it only last week in a voice filled with pride. Not the Thornton town house, for she had asked after the name of the man who employed him, but not far away either and surely folk of that ilk banded together socially.

However, when Harold came and lifted her, his strength was gratifying. Testing her legs, she found everything to be in working order and noticed Rose to be doing the same.

'I'll see you both home, miss. You still look a bit wobbly.'

The bandage about her head throbbed and Annabelle tried to loosen it a little. She hoped it was clean and that the pressure from it would stem the blood loss until she could get back to White Street and deal with it herself. With thanks, she took Harold Roberts's offered arm, spots of colour dancing in her vision.

'The healer, Miss Smith, was in an accident today in Whitechapel, my lord. I thought you should know of it.'

'An accident?' Lytton stood very still as he waited for the answer.

'A carriage hit her. It came out of nowhere and threw her on to the road, according to Roberts. He works next door in the kitchens of Lord Stephens.'

Each of his valet's words came through a beating horror.

'Was she killed?' He could barely ask this question.

'Not killed, my lord, but hurt badly.'

'Where is she now?'

'At home with her aunt, Roberts said, my lord.'

Lytton looked at the time. Three o'clock in the afternoon. 'Tell the driver to have the carriage brought around and make sure it is ready to leave in fifteen minutes.'

'Yes, my lord.' Lytton could see questions in the eyes of his valet as he turned to find his coat. What the hell would happen now?

He had deliberately stayed away from his town house yesterday morning when Miss Annabelle Smith had come to see his sister. He hadn't wanted to meet her again, here, bounded by protocol. He had wanted a clean break and a certain ending and Lucy's improving state of health had been conducive to such a plan. She was recovering. The baby was no more. She had also stated an intention to retire to Balmain Hall and Lytton was all in favour of it. He knew his servants would not gossip, but he wanted to make sure that the man who had done this to his sister would not brag either. When Lucy could speak to him without looking as if she might shatter, he would pursue it further. But meanwhile he would make his own enquiries quietly so as not to incite question.

Right at this moment there was also the further problem of an accident. What did 'hurt badly' constitute? His mind raced across many possibilities but he batted them all away. He would go and see for himself. He would visit Miss Annabelle Smith openly. He would bestow a good sum upon her clinic for discreetness and for confidentiality and to help her through this dark time and then...then he would forget her, consign her to a mistake just as he had done with all the other women he had once admired.

It would be an end to the nonsense. Lady Catherine Dromorne and he would marry and produce heirs to take the Thornton name marching into the future. A continued line of Earls.

He swallowed away fury. It was ordained. He was only a vessel for such perpetuity, a slight figure in the descent of lords who had come before him and would come after him. The tapestry of history.

His first look at Miss Annabelle Smith drove each and every thought he had had in coming here away.

She looked beaten and scared and injured. One eye was black, her head was bandaged and her wrist sported a sort of splint from the elbow to the tip of her fingers.

'What the hell happened?' He could not help the anger, roiling in without end.

'A carriage hit me. Rose was there, but she is recovered. We did not see it for it came on the end of Whitechapel Road where the street turns. Then it kept going.'

A tight corner by the sounds of it, Lytton thought. Had someone deliberately tried to hit them?

He sat when she gestured to a chair on the opposite side of the small room, three feet between them. He wanted to touch her, hold her tight in his arms against his chest to banish the demons so plain in her face. He wanted to tell her, too, that she should leave here and come to somewhere safe and beautiful. To rooms similar to those he had procured for Susan Castleton.

That thought had him flushing. He could not offer Miss Annabelle Smith that and she would never accept it.

They were caught here, in limbo, Whitechapel throbbing outside her door and her aunt in the very next room. Caught by circumstance.

'Did you see who was driving, who was inside?'

'The driver wore livery.'

'Hell.' He saw her grimace. 'I promise it was not mine.'

For the first time a smile threatened. 'I did not ever think that.'

A new silence lay in the room as they both sought direction. Lytton could see that she was worried, he could see her lip quiver and that her wide blue eyes were bruised.

'I think...' She stopped.

'What?'

'I think someone has been following me. I have never really seen him, but I feel it. Someone dangerous. Someone who wants me gone.'

'Gone?'

'Dead, perhaps. Dealt with. Banished.'

At that he stood, being careful not to trespass upon their distance. Once breached, he was unsure exactly what might happen next.

'I will employ someone to walk with you. Someone large.'

She shook her head. 'I don't want to be a prisoner.'

'You also do not want to be dead.'

'Everyone will talk.'

'About what?'

'About you paying for a protector. There are woman here who have such men...'

'Annabelle.' It was the first time he had ever used her name.

'Yes.'

'There are two things that you can now do. Listen to gossip or feel safe. Which is it to be?'

'I want to be safe.'

'Good. There will be someone here for you in the morning. He will stay close until I have caught whoever it was who ran you down.'

'How could you do that? How could you find them?'

'Easily.'

She believed him for his troth was not lightly given. He looked tired today, the gold in his eyes clouded. He looked big, too, his strength easily seen and the power that sat on his shoulders well in evidence. She needed this strength even though she could not understand his promise.

'I would not be able to pay you for such a guard.'

'I would not expect you to.'

'And I won't use blackmail to get what I want. Ever.'

'I know that, too.'

This conversation was going everywhere, running across the threads of what bound them together. Lucy. Medicine. Respect. *Desire.*

That last realisation made Belle blush and she sought for pragmatism and logic. Why was Thornton here? She could not ask. She could only sit and wait until he left.

'I am sorry.' His words held echoes and it was as if he had read her mind. Again.

Then he was gone.

Chapter Eight

Lytton drove directly from Whitechapel to the home of Aurelian de la Tomber. His friend was more than interested in the story he told.

'So the driver wore livery?'

'Of gold and blue. And the horses were a grey pair. Roberts, a kitchen hand on the scene, had noticed them go past a few seconds before the accident. His mother, who was with him, said the curtains in the carriage were drawn.'

'The clues mount. We'll have this bastard in no time. What will you do with him.'

'Kill him with my bare hands the way I am feeling at the moment.'

'Is Miss Smith hurt badly?'

'She has a cut on the head, a black eye, two torn-off nails and a badly broken wrist. The skin across her cheek has been grazed and she is damned frightened.'

Lian whistled. 'This from a Boadicea who by public gossip is scared of nothing?'

'You have been asking after her?'

'Shay thought it wise. He said you were staring at her that morning as if she were the Holy Grail. He wondered at her story.'

'With friends like that who needs enemies?'

'Rumour also has it you will be marrying Lady Catherine Dromorne very soon.'

'I am.'

'While riding all over London in the hope of saving a woman who means nothing to you?'

Breathing out at that, Lytton laid one hand across the solidness of a mantel. 'Nothing is ever simple.'

'Try to explain it, then. I am here to listen.'

He took a breath and started. 'Annabelle Smith is brave and beautiful. She is also in need of a saviour.'

'Which is you?'

Nodding, he wondered at such honesty. 'There is something about her that is remarkable. Some sense of honesty and purpose and truth...'

'Shay says the opposite. He says all he could see in your healer was secrets.'

'She has those, too, but I think they are not hers. I think someone else has forced them upon her.'

'Merde,' Aurelian swore. 'I thought Violet and Celeste were mysterious and complex, but this woman...'

'I think someone from her past is now trying to kill her.'

'Why?' Lian suddenly focused.

'Because she is not as she seems. Because she is visible. Because she has escaped from the safe boundaries of Whitechapel and stumbled into my world.'

'So now you feel you are responsible?'

'Perhaps, for the one who wants her harmed is here, close.' Through the wide windows of Aurelian's study Lytton could see London town, the rooftops varied and the trees of summer green. It was raining again. Lately, he thought, it had scarcely stopped.

'Maybe you are right. They make sense, your

deductions, the change of circumstance, the flighty darts of fate. Who are your enemies, Lytton?'

'There are many. Business fosters losers who hate a winner. Gambling is the same and jealousy is a hard task master. The list is as long as your arm and as varied.'

'Then write the names down and I will cross each off as I look into their recent movements and the state of their stables. Surely a near miss would leave some sign upon the body of a chassis or in the paintwork and footmen and drivers can always do with an extra bob.'

'I'll ask at Tattersall's. They might recognise the description of livestock.'

'Do it carefully though, Thorn. If the bastard knows you are enquiring after him he will use the time to hide his trail and if the driver was indeed liveried he will have the means to do it.'

'I appreciate this help, Lian. Could you keep all this confidential for now?'

'When can I meet her? Miss Annabelle Smith?'

'You never will. She is not for me.'

'If you say so, Thorn. Have a drink then and tell me more about Lady Catherine Dromorne.'

Lytton lay in bed that night, wondering about Annabelle Smith's safety. He had hired a man recommended to him by Lian under the instructions to be there at White Street in the early morning. He could not think after the near miss today that the perpetrator would be up to trying anything more tonight.

He needed to sleep because he had hardly had any rest since this whole thing with Lucy had begun weeks before. Yet he couldn't seem to relax as images of Annabelle with her damaged face and head and hand came to mind.

God, he'd plighted to courting Catherine Dromorne in twelve weeks' time and he had hardly given her a thought. That worried him, as did the fact that he could have somehow been the catalyst for the attack on Annabelle Smith.

Had someone seen him at her house or her at Portman Square and put two and two together to make five? Did they think there was more to their relationship than simply paying for her services as a herbalist? He frowned at this. He had found himself calculating the same possibility and yet she had hardly given him any sort of carte blanche on her affections.

Rather the opposite. Today she'd looked as though she had wanted him gone for all the minutes he was there, though the same sort of spark between them had ignited as it had each and every other time they had met, the warmth of it curling into his blood.

He would not let her be hurt. He would protect her to the very last farthing of his more-then-substantial fortune and even that thought was worrying. She was an enigma, sometimes this and sometimes that and then something else entirely. His reactions to her were topsy-turvy and disquieting.

He'd gone to Whitechapel to offer money in order to have her out of his life and instead? Now she was more inveigled in it than she had ever been before and he did not want that changed.

Lian had caught on to his ambiguity and had known that Annabelle Smith held more than his mere respect. If he carried on in this way, others soon would, too.

The moon was out tonight, almost full. He wondered if she saw it from her room in Whitechapel as it hung high above London, shining on all the various facets of it. Did she find sleep in her pain or was she lying there as he was, sleepless with thought?

Could he ever regain the sort of life he had had before he had met her? The life where he had barely glanced at another in terms of for ever.

God. That truth had him sitting and reaching for the brandy bottle by the side of his bed. Business was brisk and required all his attention. Lucy was in need of him with her loss of the child and in her bid for freedom. His brother had been sent down from school and was due at Balmain come the morrow and God knew where Prudence was, running from it all in the far-flung parts of southern Europe.

He could not be thinking of a healer from Whitechapel who should mean nothing to him and could only cause trouble. Yet he was and there wasn't a thing he could do about changing it.

He slept fitfully and in small bursts and was glad when the dawn came and he could finally get up.

Belle looked at her face the next morning and grimaced.

Her left cheek was red raw from scraping the road and the eye that had blackened was now swollen and sporting other colours of purple, red and a dark crimson. Her hair was still matted from the blood she had lost and the bandage had left deep ridges in her forehead when she unwound it. At least it had stopped bleeding and the pounding headache of yesterday had subsided to a lesser ache.

She could not believe the Earl of Thornton had come again. She was astounded by his offer of a guard and his direct and honest manner with her. They had not touched. She was glad of that because in her shock and fright she knew if they had she might have simply clung on to him and held there, like a limpet to a rock in the face of a storm-filled sea that was sweeping her away.

Thornton made her less and more all at the same time. Less careful, more trusting, less certain, more aware. He stripped back the façade and found her core, trembling against circumstance and soft inside the hard shell she had wound about herself for all the years of her life.

Surviving.

Soon there would be nothing left to fight the foolish hopes that were rising each time she met him and then what might happen?

A guard was in place when she opened the curtains, a tall bulky man who stood still like a sentry, highly visible in the moving tableau all about him. People looked, of course they did, but they moved on as well because of the menacing and ominous stance. He meant business. He wanted violence. A man like that in Whitechapel was a known quantity. People stayed well away.

'Have you seen him, Belle?' Her aunt came through the doorway, her glance upon him through the glass. 'He says he will remain at your side until he is told not to. He does not expect that to happen any time soon. His name is Mr McFaddyen. A Scot, I would guess, and a Highland one to boot. Milly says he could probably snap a man in two with his bare hands if he wanted and he has the look of one that does.'

'Is this supposed to be reassuring, Tante?'

'It depends if it is the man who went out of his way to make certain his carriage hit you and Rose yesterday. If it were he, I should be at Mr McFaddyen's side, cheering him on.'

'How is Rose this morning? Have you heard?'

'Her sister came to visit a little while ago and she is doing fine. She came to enquire after your well-being.'

'Did you tell her I was much better?'

Her aunt shook her head. 'Are you, Annabelle?' Those words came with an underlying sorrow and as a direct challenge.

'As well as a person can be when someone has just tried to kill them, I suppose.'

'There were no problems before we met the Earl of Thornton. None of this kind anyway.' Her aunt's words were tinged with accusation.

'What are you saying?'

'We should leave and go somewhere else. To the north of England, perhaps. Away from these people with money and power.'

'Why? What aren't you telling me?'

'I think your parents were of the same class as Thornton. I heard gossip in the village after they had travelled through.'

Shock and pain were a poor mix. Belle felt her heart beat so fast she thought she might fall.

'So you think this has something to do with... before? This threat?'

'I do not know, but if it is it could be perilous to all of us.'

And then she understood more. Tante Alicia had never reported her missing in the tiny French village. The church had dispatched her and Alicia had kept her, not allowing a word to go to the authorities or to the law. There would be no trail to follow if anyone happened to be looking, no true identity that could be argued. She had become Annabelle Smith at the turn of fate and stayed that way. Such actions would have placed her aunt in jeopardy should a proper search have been made. But it hadn't and surely after all these years it would never be.

Could someone have recognised her because of her visits with the Thorntons? Would that be even possible? A child of four or five looked very different from a woman of thirty-two. Her hair had darkened, for one thing.

But Tante Alicia believed she had been recognised and that was what was important. Belle now needed to reassure her that she would stay out of harm's way and remain resolutely in this crowded part of Whitechapel where strangers were noted and danger would be lessened by familiarity. No more strolls to the far end of the Whitechapel Road, no more sojourns towards the city markets and beyond.

'If anything happens again, we will leave immediately, I promise it, but I do not want to be chased away after we have made a life for ourselves here. To begin all again anywhere would be hard.'

'But not impossible.' Her aunt's voice was strained.

'No, you are right. Not impossible.'

'And you will stay here inside today?'

'Yes. I hardly feel up to anything else, but at least the bleeding has stopped and my wrist feels less painful.'

'I don't think it's a break. It holds more of the feel of a bad sprain. In a week we will remove the splint and the hair at your temple will grow back in the patch that I have shaved.'

Belle smiled and moving forward, wrapping her arms about her aunt in the best fashion that she could.

'It will all be fine, Tante Alicia. Perhaps it was just some terrible mistake...'

She stopped as a shout echoed from outside, the neighbour in the adjoining lodgings hailing them from the doorway.

'I have fresh milk and herrings for you, Miss Smith, and Mrs Drayton from down the road managed to procure farm eggs from the market in the Old Spitalfields. She said the Pauls, from across the street, will send over hot bread at noon and that the child's mother who you helped with the boils last week is promising you a mutton stew. A veritable feast, if I say so myself.'

When Belle looked across at her aunt there

were tears in her eyes. Perhaps it would be all right, after all. She accepted a cup of tea from Milly with a smile.

In the morning Lytton was again in White-chapel and was pleased to see Mr Angus Mc-Faddyen standing outside the front door of the downstairs lodging in White Street.

He had meant to simply send a message to state the sort of hours and conditions he wanted the guard to adhere to, but had found himself fretful of the passing time and so had called a carriage instead.

'Has it been quiet?'

'It has, my lord. Many have passed, but none have come close to the house at all. The women inside have insisted on feeding me every hour and the sun is about to shine.'

'Stay here until another comes. I have found a night guard to relieve you so that you can sleep and be back every morning at five.'

'Very good, my lord.'

Thus satisfied, Lytton knocked and the door was opened almost instantly by the same maid who had handed him the cup of tea on his very first visit here. She was wiping doughy hands on her apron.

'Your lordship,' she said, bobbing in a quick curtsy. 'I shall take you through to Miss Smith.'

Annabelle's eye this morning was all the hues of red, dark and light. It was also so swollen the blue in her eye only showed through a small slit of skin. Catherine Dromorne's perfect sort of beauty was once all he had liked and admired. Now he was even starting to question that. Her hair was down, which was unexpected, and fell in long, dark, curling swathes to her waist. She did not look even slightly bothered by the fact that it was unbound in his company, something every other woman of his acquaintance would have.

'I hope I find you well, Miss Smith?'

He had used her first name yesterday, the informality of it rolling off his tongue. Today he didn't.

She nodded and placed the bowl she'd had in her hands beside her on the sofa, a sharp knife and a cloth joining it.

'I am much recovered.' She made no effort at all either to conceal her bruises and he liked the fact that she did not. *Take me as I am*, such an action seemed to shout. *This is me.*

'How is your broken wrist?'

'I do not think it is broken, after all, which is a relief. My aunt is certain I have been left with only a bad sprain.'

'And your head?'

'Is fine.'

The catalogue of her wounds was not something she looked like she wanted to speak about further.

'How is Lady Lucy? Is she up and about yet?'

'She is, indeed. My sister will retire to Balmain, our country estate, next week. Mama will no doubt nurse her to death and she will be scurrying back to London as soon as she is able. So life goes on, different but still possible.'

Word of his mother brought a darkness to her eyes, but he had no inclination to try to explain his complex family life, so he left that topic alone altogether.

'I have instructed people to begin the search for the carriage that hit you. I hope to have an answer back in a few days.'

'So quick?'

'The guard outside will be here until I have found the person responsible. At night there will be another just as competent to replace him.'

'Thank you. Mr McFaddyen's presence has indeed offered us some support.'

He could see she had slept badly, for the ring beneath her uninjured eye was dark. He could also see she had been pummelling medicine with a pestle and mortar, a dark red paste sticking to the side of the bowl.

'It is turmeric mixed with castor oil. For boils,' she explained when she saw him looking.

She had not stopped work, then? She had not lain down on her bed and allowed others to wait on her. It was a lack of money, probably, and the need to make a living. If he imagined she would accept it he would have laid all the pounds he carried in his pocket on the small table beside her. But he knew that she would not and he didn't want another argument over money. How were she and her aunt paying the rent on this place then without work? Did they have savings put away to cope with situations like this one?

The ridiculousness of that thought made him frown. How did one take steps to prepare for a killer? There was so damned much he wanted to offer her and so little he could. Catherine Dromorne's face hovered on the edges of his worry, too.

'I have instructed the kitchen staff in Portman Square to put together a box of food for you. A boy will deliver it this afternoon.'

She shook her head. 'When there is trouble in places such as this people band together. Already this morning we have been brought more food than we can store.'

'Then what of the rent? How can I help with that?'

Instead of answering, she began to speak again. 'This is not your fault we have come to such a pass, your lordship. We will not refuse the guard, but any other assistance is unwarranted. You have already overpaid dearly for my services to your sister.'

'Do you have a sweetheart, Miss Smith?' Lytton asked the question before he had thought, carelessly. Usually he was never that, but there was something about her that made him unwise. Some desperation to know.

She shook her head. 'Have you?'

He hadn't been able to talk with any woman as he did with her, in such an easy comradeship and a shared respect. Awareness was there, too, simmering under every single polite word like a hidden furnace, the heat around them undeniable.

'No. The Earldom was thrust upon me at a time I was not sure I wanted it. It came with scandal, bankruptcy and death. A baptism by fire, if you like, and one that has taken up all of my time ever since.'

'But you survived?'

He laughed out loud. 'I did.'

'When I came to Tante Alicia at first it was like that for me. Not on the scale of yours, of course, but I was sick and alone and in a land I did not recognise. I wasn't sure I wanted to be there, either.'

'What were you sick with?'

Lytton knew the instant her glance fell that she would not answer him, but he wasn't going to leave it there. He reached deep into his jacket pocket.

'I have brought you a gift, Miss Smith, for your recovery and for protection. I am assured by my research that turquoise also allows healing and promotes calmness. A stone of many qualities.'

The box was small and of dark green velvet with an ornate clasp of engraved gold. Belle could barely believe he had brought a present of this magnitude for her and she held back in reaching out.

'I am not sure that I should...'

He flipped the lid and a bracelet sat inside on baize, the beads of a colour of pure green-blue, but veined in smoke. She had never seen anything quite so beautiful before. She almost wished she had not liked it so that she could have shaken her head with feeling and insisted he took it back.

As it was the words of refusal just would not come.

'Its true value lies in history. It was worn by the second Countess of Thornton when her husband the Earl took her to London to visit the Queen.'

'Like the cat in the nursery rhyme?'

He smiled.

It was expensive, then, perhaps even priceless. 'If you ever want it back...'

'I shan't.'

She was now in a quandary, the danger of touching him felt in each part of her body should she reach over and take it from his hand. She was pleased, therefore, when he leaned over and put the box on the sofa beside her.

The bracelet fitted perfectly, an amulet alive with beauty. Even with her two torn-off nails and rough grazed skin her hand looked prettier, more feminine.

'I will always wear it.'

'Good. Let's hope the healing properties begin to work their magic, for you look like you are in need of it.'

'I have nothing to give you in return.'

'You saved my sister's life.'

'Does she speak of it much? The baby?'

'Not yet.'

'Don't push her, then. Let her tell you all of

it in her own time. People need to think about things sometimes before they can work out exactly what it is they want to say to others.'

'I do not imagine she will say anything to me knowing that I'll want to kill the man who hurt her.'

'To throw away your own life for someone who is not worth it seems impossibly futile.'

Her new bracelet was warming against her skin, the day outside was finally clearing and the Earl had visited her now for two days in a row. She'd wanted life to be easy and safe and for this minute it was, a guard in place and the promise of another tonight, her aunt having a nap and Milly in the kitchen making pies.

But it was Lord Thornton who made her feel the safest, for he was shelter from a world that had turned upside down. He was a good man and strong, like those fairy-tale heroes she'd read of in books.

He stood now, hat in hand, but did not move closer.

'If you ever have need of me tell McFaddyen or send a note to Portman Square and I will come. When information arrives to hand about the carriage and its occupant, I will let you know. I promise it, no matter who is behind this.'

'Thank you.'

He looked as if he wanted to say more, but had thought against it, merely tipping his head before he left, the doorframe too low for his height so that he needed to duck down.

Belle smiled. Nothing fitted him here in Whitechapel and yet he was not out of place. She could see his danger as much as she could see the refined and elevated lord and was glad for it.

The Earl of Thornton had no sweetheart. That small information brightened her day and she brought her good arm up so that she was able to look more closely at the gemstones in her bracelet.

Why had he given her this? It seemed an excessive gift for attending to his sister. It had also been well chosen, the fit perfect and the colours exactly her own. She had never before had any jewellery and the delight of it warmed her.

Her mother had worn jewellery. For just a

second through time she remembered a finger with an ornate blue setting and a chain of gold around a thin white neck. Closing her eyes, she tried to bring the vision back, conjure her up, this mother who had passed through the small village of Moret-sur-Loing and left her there. But there was nothing. She had gone.

She could not believe she had spoken to Thornton of her sickness and of her displacement in a new and foreign land. She could see him storing each new fact learnt about her past and building a picture. Would that be dangerous? Her aunt had intimated it might well be and she might not be wrong.

If the man who had tried to kill her was close and watching, then it stood to reason the Earl could also be a target. For helping her. For placing guards. For being so very visible.

Perhaps this was why he had come today, to try to lure this other away? But he had brought the bracelet, too, in its velvet box on a bed of green baize, the catch decorated with a gold mark. An expensive piece denoting worth and from the hallmarks of history.

The woman who had worn this had gone up

to London to visit the Queen. Elizabeth the First, perhaps? Had her missing parents' relatives been among those received at court? So many questions and so few answers. But they were coming, she knew they were, and this bracelet was only a part of the knitted fabric of memory.

Lytton could not settle.

He had tried to read, tried to write, tried to beat out a tune on the piano in his bedchamber, but none of it was working. He felt wound up and furious, all the clues to the carriage that had tried to knock down Annabelle leading to nothing. Tattersall's had no knowledge of the livestock, the stables close by had not rented a carriage to any liveried riders and no one had remembered seeing the conveyance pass through Whitechapel Road or Aldgate or further afield at the time of the accident.

He was still out there, the bastard, untouched, laughing probably at his cleverness in covering up his tracks. Even Aurelian hadn't been able to find out anything and as one of the greatest spies of all time that was saying a lot.

Lytton had left the brandy alone tonight. He didn't want to drink. He needed his wits sharp and his intellect ready. He wished he was still there with Annabelle Smith in Whitechapel, sitting right next to her to make sure that she was safe.

The bracelet had suited her. It was part of a small set of jewellery that had been passed down to him from his grandfather when he had turned twenty-one. Special valuable pieces. Pieces more likely destined to be given to a wife, perhaps? He swore under his breath, castigating himself for the hundredth time that he had ever given his ridiculous promise of courtship to Catherine Dromorne. He knew he should not have.

The future skewered into different pathways and he could find no road to take that might lead to the sort of life he wanted.

Chapter Nine

He saw Catherine Dromorne and her family at the soirée of the Shaybornes three days later. It was a small gathering and as soon as he saw Shay he understood why they were there.

'My wife says it is better to know the reasons for the choices you have made. We want to see you happy.'

'And who would say I am not?' Suddenly the anger in him rose.

'You do not look happy, Thorn. Lately it seems as though you have the world upon your shoulders, but here is Lady Catherine Dromorne and I know she is waiting to talk to you.' He looked over at her pointedly and smiled.

With no other option Lytton joined the Dromorne group and Catherine fastened on to him.

'I am sorry the rumours are abounding about

our promise to marry, Thorn. My father let it slip and so...' She stopped, her face a picture of innocence.

'There are always rumours, Catherine, but I am presuming no one save the parties concerned has the full story. It might be difficult otherwise.' He tried to moderate his tone, but wondered if he had done a good enough job when he saw her frown. A dainty frown in a heart-shaped face that would make any other man melt.

'I do not wish for difficulty. Mama and Papa have enough of those—'

Their conversation was cut short as her mother joined them. The Countess of Dromorne was an arresting woman and Lytton had heard all the stories of her first Season in society. She had been incomparable and her daughters had taken after her, though he doubted that they had quite reached the heights she so obviously had.

The blonde perfection of mother and daughter was striking and Lytton found himself looking for flaws that must after all be present, though he found none.

'My husband and I are pleased for the commitment you are showing to Catherine, my lord. I know your mother must have been thrilled as well, as this union was something we had spoken of together when our daughter was first born.'

Lytton had not told Cecelia anything at all about the understanding between them, preferring to push it under the carpet until he had to face it or at least until he saw his mother next and could try to explain.

'My younger daughter Jane is due out this next Season, so it is always a pleasure to get one child well seen to before the other arrives.'

Relief rather than pleasure was evident in her voice and Lytton was grateful when refreshments came and she turned to help herself.

Catherine, however, hurried on to another topic. 'I hear that your sister is so much better for although she was a few years behind me at school I always liked her. Mama is a friend of Lady Isabel Franklin, who lives near Balmain, so we receive the gossip about your family.'

Not all of it, Lytton hoped, and accepted a glass of white wine from the passing footman.

Visions of Annabelle Smith in the carriage came with force, her hand in his, her smile uncertain, the dimples in her cheeks so deep that they contained shadows.

He could see Aurelian watching him from over in the corner, but there was nothing else he could do but concur that he had lost the battle and that unless something extraordinary happened he would have a wife in tow by the end of the year. A wife that he liked, but would never love. A wife that would suit the Earldom admirably, but would never hold his heart.

Catherine herself looked less worried as he continued to bide at her side, talking to him of her latest foray into the world of fashion and of a horse she had recently procured.

'I heard you had won a beauty yourself, Thorn, and from Lord Huntington. I imagine he would not have been happy. He has gone back to Highwick Manor to face his grandmother, by all accounts, for it was her steed. She is a woman of opinion and steel, the Dowager Countess, and not one I would like to cross. Do you know her?'

He didn't. He had no real knowledge of Huntington's family at all.

'Oh, well, enough of them. Mama feels we should have a party in three weeks at our town house. An invite will be coming your way and I hope you might stand with me in the receiving line.'

To announce his intentions to everyone present, Lytton thought, vowing to be out of London for that occasion. He was not ready for this, for any of it. All he wanted was to go home and try to work out when and where his direction in life had gone so terribly wrong.

'I hope, Catherine, that you do realise I see you as a friend. I have never held stronger feelings.' He knew this was hardly the place to have this sort of conversation, but time was running out and he needed her to understand.

Catherine shook her head and waved the words away. 'Well, who has really, Thorn? Look around you. This love that people speak of is a myth, I think. If one can get on in a marriage and enjoy friendship, surely that should be enough?'

'The Shaybornes have more, I think, and the de la Tombers.'

'Two couples out of a hundred and who really is to say it will last? Please, Thorn, we have never once had a disagreement. We laugh at a lot of the same things. Our parents are friends and we have had a most similar upbringing.'

He could not dispute that and yet in all the sentiment he understood a loss.

When a friend of Catherine's came over to join her he made an excuse and was able to extricate himself from further talk. Celeste Shayborne took his arm as he passed her by.

'You seem to be spreading yourself thinly of late, Thorn. I seldom see you any more.'

'The curse of being busy, I am afraid. The cannery business is time consuming.'

'So are women, I should imagine? Annabelle Smith was certainly interesting. And beautiful, too. I have heard you have been a regular visitor in Whitechapel ever since?'

'A carriage knocked Miss Smith over. I was seeing if she needed help.'

'My God. I had not heard of that? Is she all right? Does Summer know?'

'No, he doesn't, for it just happened and, yes, she lived, but with bruises and scratches.'

'Who wanted her hurt?' Lytton could see her mind working. Celeste Fournier had once been a spy in Paris and for her nothing extraordinary was ever simply chance.

'I am trying to find out. Lian is helping me.'

'I can't imagine someone like Annabelle Smith having enemies unless...'

'Unless what?'

'Could he have materialised from the time she does not wish to talk about?'

'I am certain he has.'

'Then what has changed lately? You? You have come into her life? Could he know you?'

'That is a good point, Celeste, and I will think about it.'

'If Annabelle Smith wants to talk to me about her past, I would be very happy to listen. God knows my own was hardly exemplary.'

'She barely talks to me of it, Celeste, so I doubt she will want that.'

'But she will talk when you earn her trust. Besides, when we met her I saw her watching you with something more than mere interest in her startling blue eyes, something more akin to worship.'

'I doubt she would agree with your assessment of her feelings.'

'I knew in a moment that Summer was the one for me, the one I would love for ever. A good union is like that, Thorn. A poor one only emphasises what is missing.'

'Thank you for your advice, Lady Shayborne.'

Celeste laughed at his tone and finished her drink.

Lytton returned home in a worse mood than he had ventured out with. He'd hardly wanted to spend any time with Catherine and her family, skirted around the best intentions of his friends and allowed Celeste to plant the hope that perhaps Miss Annabelle Smith really did think more of him than she was showing.

And a foolish hope it was. Miss Smith had not uttered anything that could be construed as vaguely personal and she had always looked thankful as he had left her company.

Even the bracelet had been a poor idea. In

Whitechapel it would probably be stolen and then pawned, no one having the slightest idea of what the thing was really worth. Or she might wear it only once or twice because she had promised it. Miss Smith gave the impression of a woman who would keep promises no matter how irksome they might become to her.

All in all, he had sold his soul to pragmatism and reaped the reward of compromise. He was miserable.

He noticed the rapping bang on the front door just before midnight and tipped his head to listen. The butler was saying something loudly and the visitor was shouting back in a voice that was louder still.

Fire was one of the first words Lytton heard and he stood. Where? Here? He sniffed at the air and could detect no scent of smoke. Feet were running now towards the library and he crossed the floor to open the door before the knock came.

'There is someone here from Whitechapel, your lordship. Mr McFaddyen I think he said his name was and...'

Lytton was out of the door before his man

was even finished speaking, striding towards the front lobby and the dishevelled and ash-covered giant who stood within it.

'What's happened?'

'The house went up, my lord, in a flash. It were started under the front door and spread like wildfire.'

'Did she get out? Miss Smith and her aunt? Are they safe?' He felt as though time was suspended, the ticks of the grandfather clock to one side slowing and the roar in his ears muffling any sound left. Like running through water, but on land. Drowning.

'They are, Sir, but only by a whisper and there is nothing left of their possessions. They are in the carriage outside. I brought them here 'cos I didn't know what else to do.'

The world refocused and Lytton walked out into the night to find Annabelle sitting on the carriage seat with the door open and watching the sky. Her aunt was fast asleep beside her, wrapped in the only blanket between them.

'Hell.' He could say nothing else as the tears she had held on to suddenly flowed down her cheeks at the sight of him, clean runnels of skin showing where soot had just been.

'I did not want to come, but...'

Lytton looked back at the house and made up his mind.

'Stay inside the carriage and I will be right back.'

Thornton House would be too much of everything for two women ripped from Whitechapel by fire and standing in the dirty rags of what was left of their clothes. The servants would talk and Annabelle would hear all of what he wanted her not to. The ravages of snobbery would destroy her as would the blow to her reputation should he deem to invite her in with only her aunt as chaperon. And that was notwithstanding any gossip about his peculiar arrangement with Lady Catherine Dromorne.

No. It had to be somewhere else and the rooms that he had learnt Susan Castleton had vacated last week in Kensington would be the bolthole he needed. He was still paying the rent, after all, and the place was the peak of discretion when it came to the ever-changing residents. His mind whirled as he catalogued the furniture within. Was there anything untoward or plainly crude about the decor? He thought not, even though it was slightly on the wrong side of being respectable. He did not imagine Annabelle and her aunt would know enough about the more usual interior decoration of the great houses in London to be surprised by this one, so he left that there.

After retrieving the keys from his library, he returned outside. Tomorrow he would hire servants and get the place in order. Tonight Annabelle and her aunt looked only as if they needed a bath and a bed.

Annabelle watched him intently, the splint missing from her hand now and the black eye much less swollen. He could not tell if the bruising was still present, but thought not given the whiteness of her skin showing through the line of tears.

Three days since he had seen her last. It seemed like for ever.

He took the seat opposite to the women, Aunt Alicia having wakened now and sitting in a miserable bundle against the door. McFaddyen climbed in beside him.

'What can you tell me about the fire?'

'It were lit, my lord, but we saw nothing at all.'

'You were not out front?'

If it was possible for a large and ornery man to look embarrassed, McFaddyen did.

'I were inside sitting down to dinner, your lordship. The maid Milly had just left to visit her mother and Miss Smith had invited me in, for it were the last of the mutton stew I had been smelling for days and so...'

'I see.' And he did. Kind manners had undone them. Sharing the last of their meagre amount of food with the guard had allowed an opportunity for whoever it was that wanted them dead.

'How did you get out?'

'I grabbed them both and charged through the front door. The dog is missing.'

Lytton breathed in hard. Stanley. Even a hound who had ripped his pink waistcoat and barked outrageously every time he had visited did not deserve to die that way.

'We will look for him again tomorrow. Dogs have a way of escaping such things.'

Aunt Alicia looked at him directly as he said this and he saw an aching hope in her old eyes.

In Annabelle's he saw nothing. She sat there as if she were made of stone, her expression dead and her chin quivering.

'Her Bible is burnt,' the old aunt murmured in her best English by way of explanation and Lytton frowned. He had not thought Annabelle Smith was so religious.

'I can buy you another one, Miss Smith.'

She simply shook her head at that and looked away. As she moved Lytton saw the beads of blue and green around her wrist under the tattered remains of her patched-up shirt and he swallowed.

It was all gone. Stanley. The house. Her paintings. Lucy's gift. The medicines. The furniture. Their lives. Gone up in smoke in the time it might take to make a cup of tea. Her Bible was the thing she regretted the most after Stanley, a link to her mother that had only just been forged. She had slept with it beside her ever since her aunt had retrieved it from the top shelf and told her the truth of where it had come from.

And now here they were, washed up again into the care of the Earl of Thornton in the late evening and smelling like burnt logs. At least she had been wearing her bracelet when Mr McFaddyen had seized them around the waist and dragged them out. It was safe. She tucked the treasure up under her sleeve so that it would not be damaged further by the soot.

This time she could not pay him. This time, if he were to have turned them away, they would have been on the street, trying to fathom where on earth they might go next.

Oh, the nuisance of it for him, she thought. No wonder the Earl would not take them into his house, but had brought them further afield. She had not wanted to meet his glance for fear of the disgust she might see there. She wanted to be apart from it all, somewhere else, somewhere clean and free. But most of all she wanted to lie down and just sleep.

Her wrist was sore and her head ached and the cut received on her leg as she was dragged through the house would need to be tended. She looked down at the soft leather of the carriage seat and saw that the soot from their clothes had left rivers of darkness upon it. There was blood there, too.

When the conveyance drew to a halt the Earl alighted first and held out his hand and Belle could do nothing but place her fingers into his. His palm curled up, the warmth of him scalding, and she might have tripped with the shock had he not steadied her.

'Careful.'

He was close now, almost against her, his big body shielding hers from the cold of night. Her aunt was watching as was the guard, Mr McFaddyen, but even with the onlookers Belle found it impossible to let go as she began to shake.

'You are safe now. No one will hurt you here.'

But they would, she wanted to say to him, and they will, because you are who you are and I am who I am. In this one small second after disaster they had a place, hung between realities and compassion. In another moment even that would be gone and common sense would prevail.

Tears resurfaced with the grief of it and then all contact was gone as he reached for her aunt.

She stood in the street, watching the building until the others stood beside her. This area of London looked nothing like Whitechapel with its dirtied bricks and its filthy streets. Here everything was clean and there was no one around. An empty place. With trees and greenery and a park just yards away. The steps were shining and the door was made of gold.

Large bunches of real flowers were displayed in vases as they walked inside and a few scattered armchairs were carved with angels and cherubs in a style she had never seen before.

Taking a candleholder that sat on a table, the Earl ushered them up a circular ironwork staircase at one end of the hall. He looked completely at home in such a place and amid the paintings decorating the wall almost from top to bottom. Once on the landing she saw the rugs on the floor were thick, burgundy interwoven with orange and blue and cream.

Then there was a door and a key turned and they were inside a space that was twenty times bigger than their dwellings in Whitechapel. A room that went on for ever.

'I hope this will do?' The Earl's voice was

an echo as he glanced around quickly. Was he looking for something? Annabelle thought.

'It is like a palace,' Belle whispered before she realised she had, drawing herself in so that the dirt would not spoil anything here. Her aunt seemed to be doing the same. McFaddyen had stopped by the door as if he understood that his sooty bulk wouldn't be conducive at all in a place like this.

'There is a bath this way. I will have hot water sent up. The bedrooms are in there.'

One room had angels on the ceiling that had the look of a picture Belle had seen in the church at Moret-sur-Loing. They were all naked. Lamps on each side of the bed had the same general look except these were of women displaying bounteous charms.

The married couple who once lived here must have enjoyed each other, Belle thought, and smiled. Thornton for his part did not look happy at all.

'I will have the rooms looked over tomorrow and some of the pieces in it replaced.'

'It is beautiful, but if we make it dirty—'

He didn't let her finish.

'I'll pay to have it cleaned.'

It was his, this place, for people owned many more houses than they could ever live in when they were wealthy. It was a knowledge on the streets.

'We won't be here long. Friends will help...' She tailed off. Places were small and crowded in Whitechapel, but Rose would have them, she was sure of it, at least until they could get on their feet.

A knock on the door brought a wave of servants in, all carrying clothes and food and other necessities and before she knew it Alicia and she were whisked off into a bath chamber. When she returned to the main room in a borrowed nightdress and slippers both the Earl and Mr McFaddyen were gone.

The letter came first thing in the morning, by special mail.

Lytton had not been to bed, the events of the night leaving him tensed up and furious, and he knew that today would be a busy one trying to piece together exactly what had happened in White Street.

The address at the top of the page was Highwick Manor in Essex and the stamp at the bottom was from the Dowager Countess of Huntington.

I put pen to paper to ask you, Lord Thornton, if I could purchase back from you the horse you won on a game of dice at the Derwents' ball.

My grandson, Albert Tennant-Smythe, Earl of Huntington, held no true right to place this steed as surety on the gambling table for the animal was my own personal property and one bred from the line of horses my late husband brought from France.

As you might have gathered this mount was a favourite of mine and I dearly wish for it to come home. I will pay well for that privilege if you would name a sum.

I realise this request is unusual, but as the ageing chatelaine of a family who has

had their share of battles and disappoint-
ments I pray for some resolution.
Yours sincerely,
Dowager Countess Annalena Tennant-
Smythe

The woman was rumoured to have a back-bone of steel, but in these words all Lytton could see was a woman at the end of her tether because of the poor actions of her family. In that, he felt a strong and shared understanding.

Taking a fresh sheet of paper, he quickly scribbled out a message.

Returned with my compliments
Thornton

He called in his butler.

'Could you see that that horse I won at the gambling tables from Lord Huntington is sent back to Highwick Manor in Essex, Larkin? It seems that the animal did not belong to him in the first place and his grandmother would like it back.'

'I shall speak with the stable master and manage that today, my lord.'

'Could you also find out from the house-keeper how the women from Whitechapel are faring this morning and report back to me?'

'I can answer that right away, my lord. Apparently they both slept very well by the account of the maid who was stationed there overnight. However, Miss Smith had a sizeable gash on her leg and the older woman has awoken with a cough. This morning Miss Smith, accompanied by Mr McFaddyen, has returned to Whitechapel to see a friend and to look for a lost dog. A Mrs Rosemary Greene is the name of the friend by all accounts.'

God, did Annabelle Smith ever stay just where she would be safe? Did she not think that one day of rest might not be enough after the fright they had had yesterday?

'Could you call the carriage around, Larkin.'

Belle saw the carriage from a distance and knew it to be the Earl's. The borrowed dress she had on was of a brighter shade than she usually wore and her hair had been placed up by one of the Thornton maids into a style emulating the wealthy. The differences had left her on edge, her life from before gone and this new one confusing.

When the conveyance stopped the Earl strode towards her with pace and she excused herself from the company of Mrs Hammond, an older woman who lived three doors up.

'I had not thought you would have been here so early, Miss Smith?' His glance took in her clothes and hair and he frowned. The house-keeper had brought them from Portman Square for her and she wondered if perhaps the woman should not have.

'I came to see if Stanley was about, your lord-ship. My aunt is fretting over his loss.'

He ignored that and asked his own question. 'How is your leg? The one hurt in the fire?'

So he knew about that, too. The Earl did not miss much.

'Much better.'

'Yet you are limping?'

He looked towards what was left of the house, the downstairs room fire blackened and smoke damaged. No one would live there for a long while and, apart from a few pewter bowls and some cutlery in the ashes, nothing else had survived.

'You could salvage only this?'

'We might find more. When we came from France we had almost as little.'

'You told me you came to England because it was dangerous there?'

'Moret-sur-Loing was close to Paris. Tante Alicia thought I should be safer away from it all and, at twelve I thought so, too. I am thirty-two now. Ancient.' She smiled to soften the point.

'Hardly that. You must know you are beautiful.'

With her un-straight tooth and her wide eyes? But he was not joking, she also realised, the compliment given with meaning.

He did not touch her, but something changed right then in the space of a second. An acknowledgment of regard. A proclamation of intent. His golden glance bored into her own without looking away, the force in them magnetic.

'Why was the Bible you lost yesterday so important?'

A different query from what she expected. 'It

was my mother's and I don't have much else to remember her by.'

'Were her eyes the same colour as your own?'

Suddenly Belle knew that they had been and it was like receiving an unexpected gift. 'They were. I had forgotten that.'

'Sapphire-blue with a hint of grey.' His words were said softly, almost as a caress, out here in the open of White Street, out here under the regard of others about them.

Her heart tripped fast, beating in her throat. 'Thank you for all you have done for us, your lordship. I am trying to find other accommodation here, though, so you can have your rooms back.'

'Thorn. My friends call me that. As I don't use this place you can stay for as long as you wish.'

She shook her head. 'If you could put up with us for just a few days longer I am certain we will be able to find other lodgings, your lordship.'

'Thorn,' he said again and she smiled.

Chapter Ten

Even in hand-me-downs and with the bruising to one eye still apparent, Annabelle Smith was breathtaking. Her beauty was not just external either. It was also in her voice and in the way that, with the odds against her, she could still see the possibilities in life.

He would never be bored in her company.

He would never lack conversation.

He would never be able to take her to his bed and make her his wife.

The grief in that realisation nearly brought him to his knees and he imagined simply taking her by the hand and running away, from England, from the Earldom, from everyone who knew them.

The sound of barking broke the spell as a

small wiry terrier ran towards them, part of his back almost hairless and one ear singed.

'Stanley?' Annabelle's voice was choked up as she knelt down to put her arms about the wildly excited dog. 'Not all is lost, then.' When she picked him up his squirming body made her borrowed gown dirty and his tongue ran across her face.

If he forgot everything else in life, Lytton vowed he would never forget this one particular moment, out in the sun, after a fire, when life began to beat again in the face of tragedy. This was what he was missing, what he had always been missing: joy, honesty and laughter, wealth even in poverty.

'Would you ride with me in my carriage, Miss Smith, and I will take you and the dog back to your aunt?'

She looked at him for a few seconds as though deciding what to do.

'First I need to get these things.' Her hand gestured towards the meagre pile of reclaimed possessions.

'Mr McFaddyen will watch over the house

and try to find more. He will bring them to you later.'

'Very well.' She followed him over to his conveyance and placed Stanley on the seat before getting in. After speaking to his guard, the Earl got in, too and closed the door, this time taking the seat next to her.

Silence shrieked around them, only the noise of the dog licking itself breaking the tension. He could feel the line of her thigh against his own and took in a breath. He was running out of time to be cautious and to be careful. Catherine Dromorne's promised twelve weeks were being eaten up day by day and the amount of minutes he might have alone with Annabelle Smith was limited. He did not know whether he should be honest with a confession as to how he regarded her or to lead with actions.

He chose the second and took her hand in his, a small hand with two broken nails and the turquoise bracelet above it on her wrist.

He did not speak. He merely looked at her and she looked back. It was not surprise on her face he saw, but something much more intense. An ordained purpose, perhaps, or simply acceptance. Her tongue licked the dryness of her lips and she tipped her head back against the cushioned leather of the seat.

In invitation and in knowledge.

Carefully he ran one finger across her cheekbone, high and delicate, before lowering it on to her lips, tracing the outline and knowing the shape. He needed to be careful, to slow down, to not frighten her.

'Can I kiss you, Annabelle?'

Question sat in her sapphire eyes.

'I will not hurt you, I promise.'

A foot became six inches and then there was nothing between them save warmth. She still had her eyes open, the blue in them threaded with caution.

'This is just for us,' he whispered, claiming her mouth under his own and as soft as he could make it.

He had meant to barely kiss her, to see what she would allow, to settle nerves and find the boundaries. But he couldn't. One touch had released a desperation for he wanted things he'd never had before, things like honesty and trust.

Grace was there, too, and decency and charm, unfamiliar and strange.

He adjusted his angle and came in deeper, the quiet kiss becoming more fierce. And then she kissed him back, leaning closer, volatile, mercurial and surprising.

She was not the timid and restrained woman he might have expected. No, she was brave, her hand entwining around his arm and holding him there. The breath she took was shaky, but her eyes were bold, slashed in blue directness. The slam of connection intensified, his body hardening under promise.

God, he was in a carriage careening through the busy streets of London and none of the curtains were drawn. He broke off the kiss and pulled back, panic building as he realised how close he had come to losing control.

Miss Annabelle Smith was a witch after all and, closing his eyes for a moment, he tried to regain composure. When he opened them he saw she was watching him intently with a heavy frown on her brow. She gave the impression of being as astonished as he was by what had just happened.

'I am sorry.' Her words.

Laughing out loud, he laid his head back against the seat and felt relief settle.

He saw humour in what had just occurred? How could he possibly think her wantonness and her lack of restraint was funny?

'The very last thing you need to be, Annabelle, is sorry.'

She could not understand what he meant by that, but the conveyance was slowing and the building she and her aunt were currently staying in was just around the corner. Her lips felt swollen and warm, the possibility of a world opening to her that she had never before glimpsed apart from in her illicit books.

They were right, those authors, about the heat of blood and the rising of desire, each emotion tempered with a loss of self that was shocking. If the Earl had not pulled back and broken the kiss, where would it have led? Belle knew that she would have had no way of calling a halt. Even now she twisted her hands into each other to stop her reaching out, glad when Stanley crawled into her lap and caused a distraction.

What would happen next?

He had not sounded angry, but then again he could hardly be pleased, either? When the carriage stopped he reached out for the door to open it.

'I hope your aunt is pleased to see the return of her dog,' he said and picked up Stanley, waiting till she had alighted before handing the animal back to her.

He would not come in? He would say goodbye here? Would she see him again tomorrow? She could not ask. With a forced smile she simply tilted her head.

'Thank you for the ride home, your lordship.'

His golden eyes darkened as she gave him her formal goodbye. 'It was my pleasure, Miss Smith,' he answered and watched her as she went through the golden doors of the Bishop Building.

Once she was inside Tante Alicia was delighted to see Stanley.

'I think it is a sign, Belle, a sign that from now on things will get markedly better.'

Annabelle tried to enjoy her happy premonition, but then excused herself to wash up after the labour of sifting through the ashes of their former home. She needed time to try to understand the way her body had responded to the Earl's, for a distance that hadn't been there before was suddenly, a detachment and reserve that felt worrying.

Would he say anything of her behaviour to his friends? Would they laugh together about the sheer absurdity of such an exchange, feeling sorry for a woman so patently unsuitable?

Tante Alicia had seen Stanley's return as a sign that things from here could only improve, but the Earl had hightailed away with an unseemly haste and she had no idea when or even if he would be back.

Edward Tully turned up at Portman Square about twenty minutes after Lytton had returned home.

'I come bearing gifts.' He handed over a parcel.

'What is this?'

'I have purchased a ticket to go to the Americas at the end of next week and, as I am going to be away for a while, I thought you might like to have this.'

Opening the present, Lytton smiled. He had always admired a small statue that Edward had commissioned three years ago, a bronze of a horse on its hind legs whickering into the wind.

'I thought it denoted freedom, Thorn, and was keen for you to have it. You seem shackled lately by your life and this is a reminder of what it could also be.'

The muscles on the stallion were well defined and the mane of hair running down his back was magnificent.

'I'd heard you sent your winnings at the gambling table from my brother's ball back to the Huntingtons'. The gossip is that Albert Tennant-Smythe is more than furious at the gesture for it has painted him in a bad light. Be careful of him, Thorn, for he is a man of limitless anger as well as a spiteful temper. By the way, I was speaking with someone the other day and they said that Lucy had been seen in his company a few times. Did you know that?'

This was the second time he had heard this and a sharp shock reverberated down his back-bone. Why had he not followed this up before when Beatrice Mallory had informed him of it?

He knew the answer.

Annabelle Smith had taken up all his thoughts of late and was continuing to do so. He wondered if he should speak to Edward about his feelings, but decided not to. The kiss from today still burnt into his conscience and it had taken a will of steel not to follow her into her accommodation and try to discover if she felt the same.

If she did, what could he truly do about it and, if she didn't… God, it would break him. He gulped down more brandy and put one hand on the shiny surface of the bronze.

'I will look after it until you get back, Ed. It's too much of a gift to just give me.'

Edward Tully laughed. 'You have always been one of my best friends, Thorn, ever since those first early years when we were consigned off to school together. For me the statue has been a guide to a new and braver direction. I hope it might work the same for you. I also want you to take the keys of my house in case you have need of some…privacy.'

'Privacy?'

'Privacy to find out exactly what it is you do seek in a bride. A bolt hole, if you like, away from the strident gaze of society and family.'

'Thank you.' He took the set of keys and laid them down next to the statue of the stallion.

After Edward had gone Lytton collected the bronze and placed it at the front of his desk in his library. He could look at it there. Everything was changing. Ed was off to America, Aurelian and Shay were married happily and he seemed stuck.

He would visit Lady Catherine Dromorne tomorrow and talk to her. He couldn't believe she'd still want to marry him if he told her that he didn't love her in the way she deserved. He would also agree to any condition of breaking their understanding as long as it left him free.

Then he would go up to Balmain and try to find out exactly how well his sister had known the despicable Lord Huntington. If the answer was what he thought it might be, he would leave for Highwick and have it out with the bastard. Then he would return to London and offer Miss Annabelle Smith the best possibility he could.

Not marriage, obviously, but a form of something semi-permanent that might do just as well. Not a mistress, for that was too uncertain, but a long-term consort with provisions for financial redress if anything at all went wrong. Provisions to look after her aunt. Provisions to fund a clinic. Provisions to allow her independence. Provisions for children if they were to have any.

Calculated. Logical. Eminently generous.

Lytton nodded. Perhaps the bronze of Edward's was clarifying his thoughts after all and he was pleased for it. The offer of the use of his house might also come in handy.

When he went to see Annabelle Smith the next day he found her alone.

'Your aunt is not here?'

'She went with Rose and Stanley for an excursion to the park. For some sunshine, I gather.'

My God, he could not believe his luck. He thought he might have had to ask her for another carriage ride in order to find some time alone and here they were, undisturbed.

Shutting the door behind him, he leaned back

against it, trying to think of just where to begin. Her eyes were of endless blue.

'Annabelle.' She frowned a little at his use of her Christian name. 'I know yesterday you must have been surprised when I kissed you, frightened even, but—'

She interrupted him. 'I wanted to kiss you. I wanted to kiss you as much as you wanted to kiss me.'

Such an open confession made him smile. Could it be this easy? He crossed the room to stand beside her, but didn't touch.

'Would there be any chance of me kissing you again? Today?'

'There would, your lordship. I thought you were very good at it.'

'Thorn.' Why wouldn't she use his name? 'You have had some practice, then?'

When she smiled her dimples showed. 'None at all, but I can recognise competence when I am confronted with it.'

No one had ever said such a thing to him. Oh, granted, he often had praise from his lovers in bed, but it had never before been couched in quite such an endearing way.

'I have read books on such things, your lordship. I know the works of John Cleland and the Earl of Rochester among others. I also provide medicines to a man in London and he often exchanges books as payment.'

The last words were said with a tremble.

'A voyeur, Miss Smith?'

He ran his hand down her good arm, lacing her fingers into his own. The pulse in her throat was beating fast and hard. 'Then allow me to show you more than the printed pages ever could.'

Pulling her to him, he placed one arm around her so that they were chest to chest, the feel of her breasts against his own all rounded flesh and softness. God, she made him frantic and desperate without even a word.

His lips rested gently on hers and he ran his tongue across them before leaning back. 'When will your aunt be home?'

'In an hour or so.' Her voice shook, but she did not look away.

Did he mean to ravish her right here and now between the servants lingering somewhere outside and an aunt who would be home as soon as the clouds darkened the day?

She had told him an hour, but a glance out of the window said it would be more likely half that time and she would not throw her virginity away on the chance of it.

Was he asking that? Surely not?

She faltered and tried to win back confidence, but when his hand cradled the back of her head and he slanted a kiss so that he covered her mouth completely, she held no chance of refusal.

Her fingers came up to his hair, threading through the thick of cinnamon and gold and brown, an aching need building as she kissed him, finding her own pressure in the truth of what was offered. No small desire this, but the galloping heat of lust.

His tongue came against hers and she opened further, allowing an entrance, the rest of her body feeling fluid in a shift of bone and blood. The room faded as did the day along with time and inhibition.

She wanted more. She wanted what she had read of in her books at night when her aunt was asleep and she could imagine two people cleaved as one in the arms of passion.

The strike of pure want left her breathless, a feeling of warmth and desire spreading to every part of her body so that the room fell away and good sense went with it. She curled into him without restraint, his hardening masculinity egging her on. She was no longer part of this world as her breath hitched and her head fell back.

The column of her throat was thin and pale as he nuzzled in, his other hand falling to one breast, feeling the nipple firm up against his touch. She was like liquid heat, the breath of her on his face, her fingers clenched around his arms so that her nails almost stung through the cloth of his jacket.

Lifting his head, he took her mouth again, harder this time with a force that was undeniable. God, he was losing control, her thighs against his own, the thin layer of silk all that stopped him from finding her centre. He wanted to reach in and take, stamp her as his own and never let go. He wanted to lead her to her bed and make love to her till the morning in all the ways he knew how. He wanted to wrap her in his arms and place her in his carriage and make for his hunting lodge in Scotland, far away from anyone and anything.

A knock at the door brought them back and away from each other. Lytton noticed how her fingers curled around the back of the sofa re-instating balance. She looked at him as if she was in a trance, as if she had no idea of what had just happened, her chest heaving and her lips swollen.

Who the hell would be here right now? When the door opened the servant announced the arrival of Aurelian de la Tomber, his hat removed as he came into the room.

Annabelle's lips were reddened as she stood there and he knew his own arousal would be plainly evident behind the fabric of his trousers. Lian was a man who never missed a thing and his first words told him exactly that.

'I passed two women at the front of the building who seemed to be heading this way. They should be here in a moment.'

Annabelle tipped her head and left the room,

her chamber lying through a small passage-way behind them. Her absence left an awkward void.

'That was Miss Smith, I presume? I hope you are being careful with her, for she does not quite seem the sort who might weather a dalliance. Weren't these Susan Castleton's rooms?'

Lytton swore, caught in limbo between deceit and lies. He no longer knew quite what was the truth—a casual dalliance, an impermanent union, or a troth that might last a lifetime and beyond. For the first time in a long while he could not speak.

She had floored him with her response. No woman before had ever made him lose control so quickly or warmed his soul with only a kiss. He felt confused.

'I think I shall go.'

'I will come with you.'

Lian looked worried, but Lytton was too muddled to even stop him.

A moment later they were outside after descending by way of the stairs, missing Annabelle's aunt and her friend.

'What the hell just happened in there, Thorn?'

'I don't know. I kissed her and the world shifted.'

A hoot of laughter was disturbing. 'When I first met Violet all I could see was her light. What do you feel when you kiss Catherine Dromorne?'

'I haven't.'

'What? Never?'

'I haven't wanted to.'

'Well, there is your answer, Thorn.'

All the parts of him were beginning to settle again now that he was out in the fresh air. 'I don't know what you are saying, Lian?'

'Don't you? Think about it more then, Thorn, until you can understand the truth. Meanwhile I have news for you which is why I sought you out. I have heard that Susan Castleton is Lord Huntington's new mistress.'

That news had Lytton frowning. 'God, I hope she knows just what she is getting into.'

'Maybe there is some history there, for word is she has known him for quite some time. The Tennant-Smythe family are an odd mix of good and evil. The old grandmother seems a woman of character, but her two children were far from it according to all that is said of them.'

'Huntington's father was handy with his fists, I recall?'

'His name was Albert, as well, and he was a violent man. Young Albert probably felt the back edge of his hand many a time which could account for the deficiencies of his son.'

'And the other child?'

'I have not been able to find out anything of her although I do know she was a daughter called Elizabeth who seems to have disappeared off the face of the earth. The family were always quite isolated up in Highwick after the old Earl passed away and, apart from Albert Tennant-Smythe, Lord Huntington, they do not mix in society much.'

'I had a letter from the grandmother about the horse her grandson lost to me in a game of cards at the Derwent Ball. She wished to buy the steed back and implied that it was not his to give away in the first place.'

'What did you do?'

'I've sent the stallion back to her. Without payment.'

'That was generous of you though it will probably encourage talk in the *ton* about the foolishness of her grandson.'

The webs had begun to spin, Lytton thought, faster and faster and he felt a sort of sideways shift. God, his whole life of late was turning upside down and Annabelle Smith seemed to be always in the very middle of the chaos. Something Aurelian had said was niggling at him, too, and he swallowed.

'You were saying when you saw Violet the first time all you could see was her light. How did you mean that?'

Aurelian stopped walking and turned towards him. 'I knew there was something about her that drew me in, something stronger than anything I had ever known before. Something that could not be ignored. I was struck down by her in the first seconds of meeting her. It was indescribable.'

'Hell.'

'You felt the same thing, then? With Annabelle Smith?'

Lytton did not want to answer that, did not want to even contemplate it as the truth.

'Let's just keep looking for the bastard who is trying to hurt her.'

He was glad when the other nodded and they walked on.

Belle smiled as her aunt and Rosemary came through the door, though her heart was racing for she felt the shawl she had fastened around her shoulders might not hide all that she needed hidden.

The Earl was gone with his friend, away from the house and yet all she wanted was for him to come back. To kiss her again, to lay his hands upon her body and make her understand the truth of passion. She did not care that it would not be for ever. He would never marry her, but perhaps just one night of lust would be enough. She was thirty-two, after all, and she would be careful to make certain nothing would come of a union in the way of a pregnancy.

To go to her grave as a woman without once experiencing the delights of sexual intercourse suddenly seemed tragic. This could be her last chance. Her first and last, she thought next, but did not dwell on that.

Could she offer? Would he accept? And where would she be able to lie with him undisturbed?

Her aunt looked exhausted and grey. From the fire, Annabelle thought. Shepherding her into her bedchamber, she bade her lie down while she found some tea. Rosemary hovered at her side when she returned to the main room.

'Your aunt seems out of sorts, Belle. She worries about you. She feels you are in danger and that she is holding you back.'

'Holding me back from what?'

'I don't know. She never mentioned any specific thing. She just said that you need to bloom and that this is the year you will do so.'

'Losing all our earthly goods does not feel much like blooming to me, Rose.'

Rosemary laughed. 'I was speaking to Mrs Roberts about your predicament and she said she has rooms you could rent now that her son has left home. I think they are quite small, though, and the kitchen would need to be shared. Milly dropped in to see me, by the way, and sends her love. She has been offered a job in the tannery in Stepney and says she will take it now that your home is gone.'

The everyday crept into the extraordinary even as Belle tried to call it back.

She had no idea as to what to do next, which direction to take. She felt uneasy here in these rooms in the middle of London, but Mrs Roberts's rented space did not feel right either. She wanted her house back and her life back. She wanted to walk the streets of Whitechapel and see familiar faces and yet even that was lost to her now given the carriage accident and the fire. She also wondered if both events could be related and what that meant for her.

Three hours later another visitor knocked on their door and Lady Lucy, accompanied by her maid, was shown in.

'I hope it is all right to visit you, Miss Smith. I am back from Balmain for a few days and after hearing about the fire I just wanted to see for myself that you were...safe.'

'I am. Your brother has been most kind and allowed me the use of these rooms until others more suitable can be found.'

'Then I am glad for it. I will be returning to the country on the morrow, but I wanted to thank you for all you have helped me with. I thought last time we met I was rather...occupied and I hoped to set things right between us.'

She smiled and glanced at her maid standing to one side of her.

'Well, I see you are much recovered now and you certainly look to be in fine health.'

'The country air does wonders for the spirit and you should join me one day, Miss Smith. A small sojourn away from the city might be just what you need, too.'

'Perhaps.' Belle left it at that. She did not want to travel to Balmain to find the Earl there given her most inappropriate behaviour. She also did not wish to be anywhere near his mother.

As if Lucy had read her mind she began to speak of her brother. 'Thorn has news, too. He will be married to Lady Catherine Dromorne before the end of the year so we now have a wedding to plan which should take my mind off things. Thornton and Lady Catherine have been promised to each other for years, according to Mama, and she is more than happy with the union.'

The shock of such words had Annabelle swallowing. The Earl had caressed her when he had known he was promised elsewhere in Holy Matrimony? He had stood there and asked to kiss her, taking her words of consent without any attempt at honesty.

He was exactly the man she had first thought he might be in her drawing room, wearing his pink waistcoat and his fingers full of rings. Shallow. Disloyal. A rake. Looking around the room, she saw other things that had not made sense before, but now did. The removal of the intimate paintings and statues had left a discoloration of the walls beneath them that was still visible.

'Is this where your brother kept his mistresses, Lady Lucy?'

She knew it was rude to ask such a question and saw Lucy's eyes widen. The maid behind looked away, trying her hardest no doubt to simply blend in with the wallpaper.

'I do believe that it might have been, Miss Smith.'

There was a knowledge in her gold eyes that told Belle other things as well. The Earl's sister had come with a warning and with her particular donation of truth. Take it as you will, she might have said, but understand the consequences. The consequences that I had to deal with. Make your decision while knowing all the facts.

'Mrs Wollstonecraft's book has allowed me a new outlook on life, Miss Smith. The independence you spoke of is indeed a gift. Lady Luxford sends you her warm wishes, too, for I saw her yesterday at the town house. They had just had Lady Catherine and her family for afternoon tea, I believe, to welcome them into the fold.'

An intertwining *ton*, all the pieces fitting and the promises kept. How foolish she had been to think she could have ever been a part of that.

'But I have also brought you something, Miss Smith.' She turned to the maid behind her and the woman handed over a small package wrapped in brown paper. 'Thorn said most of your possessions were lost in the fire at White Street and I remembered the painting I gave you and assumed that it, too, was gone. Would you accept the twin of that one as a replacement? It would mean a lot to me if you did.'

The wrapping fell away easily, this painting done in blues and greens rather than with the reds and purples.

'It's by the very same artist, but whereas the original's title was "Autumn", this one is "Spring".'

'Thank you. It is beautiful and I shall treasure it.'

The rebirth. The rebuild. A regeneration.

Perhaps it was applicable to her situation. Perhaps now she had to find the courage to rise from the ashes of her life like a phoenix. Like Lucy herself had with the sort of bravery that Mary Wollstonecraft advocated?

Belle felt shattered and broken, the question of what happened next hanging like a sword across her head. She could not stay here, that much was for certain.

When Lucy stood and made to leave, she decided to accompany her down to the carriage, just to have a moment away from these rooms and to be out in the open air of the day. But as they came on to the street Lucy gasped and turned to grab her hand and Belle saw a man standing there a few feet away watching them. He looked vaguely familiar.

'Lord Huntington?' Lucy's voice was small and frightened and Belle's heart began to beat fast. So this was Albert Tennant-Smythe, the trickster who had stolen Lucy's virginity and left her compromised in every way.

She stepped in front of Lucy, sheltering her. 'You are not to come anywhere near Lady Lucy, Lord Huntington, for your behaviour towards my friend was appalling and heinous and, believe me, you shall be punished for it.'

He smiled at that and moved forward.

'I mean it,' she said in a louder voice now, her good hand coming up to push him back. Mr McFaddyen had gone to find medicine for her aunt after eliciting a promise that Belle would not open the front door. Now that she had she was alone in this. Still, she was hardly defenceless and if the foolish Earl wanted to create a scene on the street, then she was more than willing to give him one.

She screamed as loud as she could, a piercing

desperate cry that would bring people running. But before she could utter more than a few seconds' worth of sound Huntington had stepped forward, his hand across her mouth.

She bit down hard. Years in the tenements of Whitechapel had honed her reaction to danger and he leapt back, blood running down his fingers and ill-mannered words in the air.

'You slut. You stupid ugly pretender.'

He raised his fist and Belle pushed Lucy backwards, expecting the force of his anger to land on her as she did so. But then everything changed. The Earl of Thornton came from nowhere, barrelling into Huntington with force and sending them both sprawling on to the street beside her, arms and legs flailing and in virulent fury.

Chapter Eleven

Albert Tennant-Smythe was about to hit Annabelle. Lytton could not believe it.

He charged, but the Earl had his forearm raised, blocking his fist, an elbow ramming into Lytton's side and, as he rolled away, Huntington's hand reached under his shirt and a knife glinted in the dullness of the day. Lytton felt the stab of it in his forearm and dimly heard a scream before his other arm deflected steel so that the wicked point hit stone and the weapon skittered away.

Grabbing his hair, he slammed the Earl's head down on to the cobbles, but if he thought the bastard was finished he was wrong.

Strong legs wrapped around his own, toppling him to one side and then it was his turn to feel the thud of knuckles against the flesh of his mouth and eyes. He was blinded for a moment by blood or by the force, he knew not which, but fury held strength as well and he smashed the other in the side of the head, feeling the crunch of skin and bone. Huntington went down, his nose bleeding, his eyes closed and his body curled up around the pain. Groaning.

'Thorn?' His name said softly. 'Thorn?'

And then he was back, back in a street in Kensington in the middle of a London day, his sister crying, Annabelle looking shocked.

He let his body relax into stillness, as he took in breath.

'Thorn?' His name again. Annabelle's voice. She'd never called him that before, never used his family name in any of their many conversations.

He closed his eyes momentarily. His arm ached and he was sure one of his bottom teeth had been loosened, but his focus had been regathered by the strong sense of her.

'Take my sister home.' His first words were directed at the Thornton driver and he was glad when the man took them as an order. Within a few seconds Lucy and her maid were in the awaiting carriage and then she was gone.

The law was there even as he turned, the large group of bystanders multiplying by the moment as four Runners descended on them. Without thought Lytton stepped across to Annabelle and took her hand, bringing her to his side where she would be safe.

'You will all need to come with us, sir, to the Public Office, for we cannot allow such lawlessness on London streets.' An unfamiliar carriage had now drawn up beside them and two Runners got in. Albert Tennant-Smythe was being shepherded into his conveyance by the other two, blood dripping down his face and on to his clothes.

Lytton did not want the law involved, especially if Lucy's name was to be bandied about because of it, but there was nothing else to do but accompany the men to the station.

'I hope he dies.' He could not help the bleak desolation in his words and did not even try to temper vehemence even as the two law men opposite looked over at him.

'You found out?' Annabelle's query was quiet.

'Yes.'

The silence between them lengthened, the blood in his mouth pooling and a nausea rising. He was glad Annabelle was with him despite everything, safe for this moment from a world that had fallen to bits. He saw blood on the cream in her skirt.

'God. He didn't hurt you?'

'No. I bit him. I think it is from that.'

He laughed and was surprised by the sound of it.

Lytton Staines looked battered and hurt, the flesh around his eye blackening and his top lip split. Blood stained his fingers and his shirt was torn where a knife had ripped through the fabric to slide into the forearm below.

Belle had meant never to speak to him again, yet here she was pushing back his sleeve to peer at the wound.

'It's deep.' Her fingers pressed down and he grimaced. 'An inch or so to the left and he'd have sliced your radial artery here.'

'Then I was fortunate.'

His flat tone suggested anything but. She

wondered what might happen when they reached the Public Office, but didn't dare to enquire. At least for the moment they were away from Lord Huntington. Her fingers fisted in her lap and they sat there in silence, the two men opposite them tight-lipped and frowning.

Half an hour later they were in a room, a magistrate before them.

'What the hell were you thinking, Thornton? Attacking Huntington like that out on the street in broad daylight and in front of at least three dozen bystanders?'

'The man is an ass, Wilton.'

So they knew each other these two, Belle thought, and was comforted by the fact.

'Then why not find him in some dark corner and deal with him? Somewhere where nobody else could observe you? Somewhere the law would not have had to be involved? Somewhere justice could have taken place quietly?'

'He was going to hit Miss Smith with his big bloody fist.'

'Yes, I heard that.'

'He had a knife as well.'

'Which we have confiscated. Huntington does not seem to be talking at all. He has called for his lawyer. He does not wish to take this further. Do you?'

'No.'

'Good. I hoped you would say that. There are a number of newspaper reporters at the front door ready to pounce on you for a statement. I have arranged for a carriage to collect you at the back.'

'Thank you.'

'I should also imagine there will be unwanted talk in society, but I am certain you can handle that?'

'I can.'

'If you need any help with this privately from me, Thorn—'

The Earl did not let him finish.

'I don't, but I am thankful for the offer.'

'Very well. On my behalf the case is closed then.' He handed over a sheaf of papers. 'On your part you might like to keep the statements and names of those who supported your side of the argument. In case the Earl has other plans, you understand.'

When the door opened behind them both men shook hands, the file tucked under the Earl's arm as they followed the one who had come to show them the way out. As they turned a corner into a further passageway a woman stepped out before them, an older woman with bright white hair, two servants by her side.

Annabelle caught only a quick glimpse of her before she stepped back against the wall and shaded her face with her hand as if she was feeling unwell. The older woman's maids crowded around her in consternation as they passed. The Earl gave no sign at all of knowing the woman. Perhaps she had come for Huntington? A grandmother or a great-aunt? Or perhaps she was here on other business altogether.

Annabelle was glad when the carriage was suddenly before them and there was no sign of others anywhere.

'Where do you wish to be taken, my lord?' The driver stood at the doorway, hat in hand.

'Number Twenty-Nine Bromfit Place in Kensington.'

'Very well, your lordship.'

In a few seconds the conveyance was moving and ten moments later it stopped in front of a tall stately town house.

'This belongs to a friend of mine. He has gone up north to see his family before leaving for the Americas.'

As Belle stood she thought the Earl looked wobbly. The footman hurried forward, knocking on the door, and when a servant answered they were soon inside. Lytton made straight for a sitting room of sorts, the shelves behind full of small models of planes, ships, buildings and other inventions that she had never seen the likes of before.

'Ed's passion is to invent things,' he said by way of explanation and then sat down in a leather chair by a small cabinet, helping himself to a drink.

'I would offer you one, but after last time…?'

He left the rest as a question and waited until she shook her head.

'I hope you do not mind me bringing you here. We need to talk and I thought it the most private of all the places I know.'

'The magistrate will not question you further?'

'No. Wilton is a friend of mine and can be trusted. If Huntington does not talk, then neither shall I.'

'Because it will be better for Lucy that way?'

'Yes.' His eyes were burning gold, no tenderness within them. 'Once that secret is uncovered publicly there will be nothing I can do to stop it hurting my sister. As it is Tennant-Smythe knows I know and for the moment until all this dies down I need to imagine that to be enough.'

'And after?'

He ignored that and asked her another question entirely.

'Can you sew?'

'As in clothing?' Belle could not understand just what he meant. Did he wish for her to mend his shirt?

'My skin. I think it might need a stitch or two.'

Relief bloomed. 'Yes, of course. Is there a needle?'

'Probably in the drawers of that desk over there.'

He waited till she found one, threading up the cotton and knotting one end.

'Take off your shirt.'

She saw his smile.

'I'll need hot water, too.'

The same servant as before came on the pull of a cord and the Earl asked him to bring water, flannels and bandages.

When he placed the bottle he'd held down on the table between them she picked it up. 'This will keep things clean.'

Overturning the liquor into a kerchief from her pocket, she waited until it was soaked in and pulled the needle and strands of thread through the damp material.

With his shirt off she saw that he was not a man prone to indolence. His body was well muscled, an aged scar of considerable proportion slicing down the top of the same arm that he had hurt.

He didn't look inclined to talk of it, though.

'How did you find out about Lord Huntington?' She needed to keep his mind off the pain that was to follow.

'I'd had word of my sister seeing Huntington from a few people, but then I read a letter my sister had written to him but had never sent. It was jammed into the Wollstonecraft book in her room. Huntington did not rape her, by the sound of her confessions, but he pushed her much further than he should have.'

'The familiar and unsettling entitlement of a lord.'

Belle pricked through his skin, but he did not move an inch. Knotting the stitch before taking another, she blotted away the dribble of blood. She should mention that she knew about the purpose of her accommodation in Kensington and the name of his unmentioned bride-to-be, but just for this moment he was her patient and she would leave confronting him until she had finished stitching at least.

'The Earl has always been a troublemaker. I knew him at school.'

'Your sister made a lucky escape, then.' She finished a sixth stitch and then a seventh, finally knotting the last one off and placing her linen handkerchief across the gash.

'Luck is a word that can hold many shades.'

'As does truth, my lord.'

Reaching for the roll of fabric the servant had delivered, she wound the length of it around his arm, tying it off with a divided end. He replaced his shirt immediately, buttoning the garment up to the neck with difficulty. There was sweat on his brow.

She did not help him. She would fashion a sling for him when she could, but for now...

'Your sister mentioned that you are to be married before the end of the year.'

He stilled, though the pulse in his throat quickened.

'So I was wondering how you thought it appropriate to...kiss me in the light of such a troth?'

Holding the wounded arm into his side, he stood. His eye was swelling, his lip was bleeding and there was a graze right down the side of his cheek. Yet he looked beautiful, his eyes fastened upon her, a sadness there edged in despair.

'I could not help myself and Lady Catherine Dromorne is, in truth, no more than a friend.'

'Who you have asked to marry?'

'Not exactly…'

Now anger did surface.

'How does one become promised to another in a "not exactly" way?'

'I am an earl and the position, while having many advantages, also has its drawbacks.'

'Drawbacks.'

'I cannot marry just anyone. Catherine and I have been promised from birth and it is my duty to make certain the Earldom leaves my hands in better shape than I found it in.'

'Then what am I doing here? With you? Why did you bring me here to this place?'

'Because I cannot ever get time alone with you and because there is something between us that is inexplicable. I want to know what that is. Understand it.'

'And then what? Will you proceed to ruin me and then scurry back to your suitable bride-to-be. Like Lord Huntington? Or did you mean to establish me as a mistress in your grand rooms in Kensington? A little bit on the side when you had the time or the inclination. A visit now and then when you felt like it?'

'No. It was not like that.' He stopped, giving the impression that he wanted to say more, but couldn't. 'I wanted to protect you, keep you safe...'

The weight of his words felt heavy inside her. He had done that. Time after time. After the carriage accident, after the fire, after the Earl had brought his big heavy fist down through the air in her direction.

He had protected Lucy, too, and her Aunt Alicia. He had employed McFaddyen to stand guard on the apartment and brought Stanley home from the ashes in Whitechapel.

He'd been a buffer to absolute poverty, a bulwark against homelessness and starvation. He was still being that, even now, with his damaged hand and face. But his destiny lay elsewhere, not by his command, but by the forces of history.

The anger left her in a rush and all that was left was tiredness.

'I think we shall never understand what this

is between us, my lord, but we need to have the sense to leave it alone.'

He sat at that on the chair by the window and leant back against the leather headrest. His exhaustion was palpable. The blood loss, she supposed, for the cobbles had been running with redness. Quietly she took her place opposite him, in a deep burgundy armchair, positioned at an angle to include his own.

'I will order us something to eat, Annabelle.'

He waited until she nodded before calling the servant back.

It had begun to rain outside. Belle could hear it dripping against the window. But her own world was encapsulated in here, the sense of dislocation heightened by the strangeness of the room and all the small inventions around her. The Earl waited till the servant was gone before he began to speak again.

'You pushed my sister behind you when Tennant-Smythe was about to strike. I do not know one other woman who might have done the same.'

'I am from Whitechapel, my lord. There is nothing soft there.'

'You used my name when you called to me in the fight?'

'I thought he might kill you with the knife.'

He smiled at that. 'Hardly. Shay and Aurelian taught me much about the art of defence.'

'Yet there is a large scar at the top of your injured arm?'

'That came from a mistake. I trusted the man who did it, you see.'

'Who?' A single word dragged from horror.

'My father. I had just won Balmain back in a game of cards and he was not thankful. He shot himself a few hours later. I have never told anyone those exact details before.'

'He hated you?'

'He hated himself. At least for me I have tried to behave honourably. The rooms in Kensington were all I had at such short notice and I had my staff take away anything even vaguely offensive the day after you arrived.'

'The statues and the paintings. I wondered where those had gone.'

'I have been seeking something else more suitable in the meantime, but…'

'But?'

'You do not accept help easily and it seemed such a gift might be construed as charity and as such rejected. So we are at an impasse, you and I, caught by circumstance and perhaps by lies.'

'Your lies?'

'Ours, Annabelle. Can you not feel what is here in this room between us?'

Shock held her still. He felt it, too, this connection, quivering and desperate? 'What is it?'

'Desire,' he whispered. 'Yearning. Need. There are a hundred other words I could say and all them together might still not explain it.'

'But it is there none the less.' Her words rolled into the silence as the lump in her throat made tears pool in her eyes.

Neither of them moved, the fragility of such a confession too new and too wondrous. With only a tiny mistake it might shatter, these troths of hope and faith. Such a brittle truth. Everything was too precarious with Lady Catherine Dromorne in the mix and her own lack of family. It was too soon for honesty. She stayed quiet.

The food came on a tray. There was cheese and figs and crusty bread as well as a cake and biscuits. He had asked for tea as well, the steaming aroma of it filling the air around them.

As the maid bent to pour the Earl stopped her. 'We will manage. Thank you.'

When she was gone Belle leaned to pick up the teapot, glad for something to do. He took milk and two teaspoons of sugar. She handed over the cup with care, making certain that she did not touch him, and then she poured one for herself.

She looked frightened and uncertain. She looked as if she might leap from the chair and run out the door. But the teacup at least momentarily anchored her. Lytton sipped at his own drink with distaste. He seldom drank the stuff, but she had poured it for him and he needed harmony. The sugar at least steadied him.

He wished he might simply have reached over and taken her hand, but he did not dare to. The ground he stood on was shaky and the next move had to be hers if there was to be any hope in it.

'I have had no luck with identifying the carriage that hit you and your friend on the White-chapel Road despite an exhaustive search. Whoever it was went to great measures to avoid being caught.'

'Which implies either wealth or luck?'

'My pick is probably both.'

She nodded and sat back, her feet square on the floor, her boots scuffed with age and use.

'But I will find him,' he continued. 'At least believe that.'

'Thank you.'

A silence again. Ignoring the awkward tension that swirled around them, he breathed out. When she looked up the light caught her eyes, surprising him as they did each time with the pure blueness.

'Where do we go from here?'

Her question was brave for it tackled their dilemma head on and he decided to answer in kind. 'Either you leave, Annabelle, and we never see each other again, or you stay.'

'Stay?'

'Here.'

'I cannot...'

'I promise I will do nothing you don't want me to.'

For the first time he saw her dimples.

'I won't press you for anything.'

He couldn't believe he had said that. But he meant it. If there was nothing more than the promise of a simple touch, he would accept the offer. All he wanted was for her to be there, by him.

When she nodded he felt his heart beat faster in his throat. He hoped Annabelle did not see the power she held over him.

'I have sent word to your aunt to say you are with me so that she will not worry.'

Her glance met his. 'Or she will be more worried than she was before.'

'Why?'

'She thinks you are dangerous to me in ways that I cannot fathom. She thinks all that has happened with the carriage accident and the fire has come about because of my association with you.'

'And what do you think?'

'That she is probably right. Before meeting you my life was centred around Whitechapel and healing. No one there wished for my demise. More usually they were glad for my help.'

'And then everything began to happen after you came to Portman Square to aid my sister? God, you don't think it was any of us, do you? My mother might be a bitter woman and inclined to depression and delusion, but I am certain she would not flout the law.'

Was it himself who had put her in danger by asking for her services? Had someone seen her with him and decided that in Annabelle Smith there lay a pathway to revenge? He had enemies, he knew he did, but still he could not think of one who would take things to the extent of trying to kill an innocent.

'I want to see you safe, Annabelle, in any way that I can.' The light was falling and inside the shadows gathered.

He stood then and crossed to the window, looking out over the city, at the rooftops and at the road below which was almost empty at this time of the late afternoon.

He felt at a crossroads. Take one step in any direction and his life would change for ever. He needed these next moments to count.

'Whenever I touch you I feel that I have come home.'

One tear traced its way down her cheek, falling to her gown, wetting the silk so that the yellow of it turned darker. Almost gold.

'But I am not a saint, Annabelle. Barely even a ghost of one and I confess that I have known lovers in the carnal way many a time.' Turning, he made himself say more. 'But I also swear I have never wanted a woman as I want you, never burned as I do for your touch.'

He stopped as she walked across to him, holding her fingers against his cheek in the way of a caress. He closed his eyes and he felt her warmth across his mouth and around the shape of his lips.

'I don't want to hurt you,' she whispered and for a moment he did not understand what she was saying. Break his heart? Slice away any hope?

'Your lip. It is cut.'

He smiled.

'What would happen, if I said yes? That I would stay tonight with you, here in the house of your friend?'

'Then I would have to ask you to marry me, Annabelle.' He tried to make the words sound kinder, but the shock of them arced through him, a troth he had never once before given in all the years of his life, but words torn from need and hope.

She shook her head, the dark of her curls falling across the yellow in her gown. There was a deep frown on her forehead. 'It would ruin us both and I will not be the cause of that.'

He brought her fingers to his lips, kissing them along the healing wounds on her skin. His broken lady, brave and true.

'So if I will not marry you and I cannot be your mistress, where does that leave us?'

'Here,' he answered and his lips came across her mouth, tasting and seeking, finding acquiescence, her body speaking with the words she could never say. Accepting.

His kiss this time was nothing like the others. Instead it was slow and soft and gentle. There was a sadness there, too, as if this would be the very last time he held her close. With it came an intimacy that was staggering.

Neither of them closed their eyes, the gold of his own saturated with desire as their bodies began to move together. Opening her mouth further, she felt his tongue tasting, felt his hands on her face drawing her in, felt the beat of his heart speed up to match her own. Cleaved into one. Hers. Her man. Thorn with his honour and his beauty and his braveness. Thorn with his Earldom and his family and his responsibilities.

She would not tell him she loved him, not now and not like this. But she did love him. To the very bottom of her heart and soul. She wanted the best for him. She wanted him to be happy. She wanted him to have a place in the world, in his world, the world of the *ton*.

Breaking off the kiss, she dropped her forehead against his chest. She needed to leave before she could not. Removing the bracelet he had given her, she handed it over to him.

'I cannot keep this.'

He nodded and let her go, one step between them and then two.

'You are sure?'

'We live in different worlds, my lord, and what might work at first would eventually not.

Could you live in Whitechapel, with all its customs and idiosyncrasies, in a two-bedroom house with the street at your doorstep and a thousand things that are unfamiliar and frightening and dangerous?'

'A different world from the one I'm used to, you mean? One I was not conversant with?'

She nodded. 'Portman Square is as foreign to me as is society with all its many and intricate expectations and unwritten rules and there would be so many things I would do wrong. I would be as lost there as you would be in Whitechapel, no touchstone to simply be. Then afterwards, after it all failed, to be left with regret and hatred...' She stopped. 'It would be impossible to survive such a thing. I know it.'

'I always thought you were brave, Annabelle, brave enough at least to try?'

'Brave enough to let you go, too. To wish you well in your new ventures and to hope that your life should be exactly as it was determined when you were born an earl.'

She hated how her voice had begun to shake. Another moment and he might hear it. Just one more to get through to appear to be in control.

She saw him swallow and the emptiness in his eyes broke her heart.

'The carriage shall be brought around then to take you home, Miss Smith.'

'Thank you, my lord.'

He did not put the bracelet down, but kept it in his fingers, turning the stones. Belle could feel his eyes on every part of her body. A farewell. A valediction. The tightness in her chest made it hard to take in breath.

Once back in the apartment in Kensington she went in to see Alicia in her bedchamber. Her aunt was reading.

'I received the message and did not expect you back so soon. Are you all right, Belle? You look pale.'

'What happened with the man in your life, Tante Alicia. The one you loved when you were young?'

Her aunt sat up and carefully smoothed out all the creases on her sheet before speaking. 'He married another and they lived happily ever after. When he left my heart was shattered and it was a long time before it began to mend. I could not suffer that twice, so I made it my mission to never cross his path. My family had lost its place in the world, you see, any lands and houses we once owned were gone and we were largely shunned by society. I had no position left to be in his life, no way of becoming the woman he needed.'

'Yet you were well brought up? You were hardly a poor match for him? Did he ever try to see you?'

'Many times. It was, in truth, part of the reason that we came to England.'

Breathing out, Belle put her head in her hands.

'The Earl of Thornton almost asked me to marry him today.'

Alicia's concern was obvious. 'What answer did you give him?'

'That I could not. That I would never fit. That I would ruin him if I was to ever say yes.'

Old hands came to cover her own, the age spots easily seen. 'I think that was the right decision, Annabelle.'

'Do you?'

'Yes. You did just as I did. You are allowing

the Earl to live his life as it ought to be lived. The life he was born to. The life he would miss for ever if you had only thought of yourself.'

'But it hurts. Here.' She placed her hand across her heart.

'It would hurt more to see the Earl's possibilities dissolve before your eyes. He would say it did not matter, but in the end it would. Then there would only be blame and hurt. You would see it in his eyes when he could no longer hide it and hate yourself for it. Just as I would have done had I followed my heart.'

'I think we should leave here tomorrow early in the morning. Mrs Roberts has offered us a room. Just for now it would be a good start and then who knows where we might go.'

'I will get up and pack our things. At least after the fire we do not have much.'

Alicia's voice shook as she said this. Another move at her age difficult and unwanted and Belle felt a further arrow dart into guilt. If she were not to survive this...

'None of this is your fault, my love, and I will be perfectly fine, so stop worrying.'

The ghost of relief was there as she turned to

her own room to find her things. Thorn had not asked her to marry him from love, she thought. Lust was more of a reason and the sheer want to keep her with him, two people from completely different worlds who somehow had been drawn together.

Then I would have to ask you to marry me, Annabelle.

Those were his words when he had realised she might stay. A duty. The honourable thing to do. There was nothing of adoration in such words, nothing of the things she felt at all. The Earl of Thornton had uttered them only because it was the right thing to do.

She folded the few clothes she had in a bag along with the painting Lady Lucy had insisted she take and then she sat down on the large bed and closed her eyes.

'Help me,' she whispered whether to God, her mother or the world in general she knew not which. Then she breathed in deeply three times and stood. Whatever happened next she would survive it because the worst of all possibilities had just taken place. No one and nothing could ever hurt her again as badly as Thorn just had.

Chapter Twelve

Lytton did not go straight home, but made a diversion to White's to sit for a while in the quiet of the place and simply be. When Aurelian came over he almost thought to leave but decided against it, his friend's smile full of concern.

'You look exhausted, Thorn. From business or from love?'

'Love?'

'It is becoming known around town that you have installed a new mistress in the rooms vacated by your last one.'

'Who is saying that?'

'One can barely move in the *ton* without eyes watching and as Miss Annabelle Smith is more than beauteous she is a worthy target.'

'She is not my mistress. I tried to ask her to marry me, but she refused.'

Lian began to smile. '*Mon Dieu*, Thorn. You have what?'

'You heard?'

'*Mon Dieu*, but how the mighty have fallen. I thought you always said that you would only marry for convenience? This situation is hardly that.'

'Which is the problem. Miss Smith feels our worlds would never fit. She turned me down because of it.'

'To protect you? She sounds like an angel.'

'I think she is.'

'I can't believe this is you speaking? Wait until I tell Violet. Does Shay know?'

'No. You are the first person I have seen since her refusal.'

'So what now?'

'I need to talk with Catherine to break off any agreement between us. I also need to talk to the old aunt of Annabelle's, for I think she does not trust me and I can't quite understand why. After that I will go to Rundell's and purchase the most beautiful sapphire ring that I can find. Perhaps that will convince her of my sincerity.'

'Women want the words, Thorn. I don't think a priceless bauble is quite what the unusual Miss Smith would desire.'

'What words?'

'Talk to Violet or Celeste before you make your next assault. They will let you know exactly.'

'I might just do that. Is your wife at home tonight?'

Aurelian's laughter worried him.

The Dowager Countess of Huntington, Annalena Tennant-Smythe, graced Lytton with a visit two days later. As a woman who seldom left her home in Essex he was astonished to find her calling card in his hand.

'Put her in the blue salon, Larkin. I will come immediately.'

She was far smaller than he imagined and when she looked up at him Lytton felt a shock of astonishment. This was the same woman who they had passed outside Wilton's office as they'd left and she had Annabelle's eyes. The same colour and shape. The same startling blueness with grey just at the very edges.

Was he going to see Annabelle in everyone now that she had disappeared, packing up her things from his apartment and gone to God only knew where?

Whitechapel, if he could guess but unless she wanted him to find her he knew that he would not be able to locate her for all the looking in the world. The place had its own sense of loyalty and in the alleys and the small joined narrow roadways people could be hiding for ever.

'My lady. It is a pleasure to welcome you here.'

The woman turned directly towards him, her prim figure outlined against the large window behind. 'My grandson by all accounts tried to kill you, Lord Thornton, and I have come to apologise for his foolish and dreadful behaviour. He almost struck a woman in public, too, it is being said and I presume she was the woman I saw you with at the Magistrates Office? There are whispers he hates you for returning my steed to me at Highwick, which was a kindness that I cannot thank you enough for.'

'You do not need to apologise for the Earl. It is his shame.'

'No. It is also a family shame and, believe me, the Huntingtons have had more than their share of scandal.'

'My family is much the same.'

At that she laughed and deep dimples graced each cheek. Another reminder of Annabelle. He reached for the brandy and offered her a drink.

'Oh, I never drink alcohol, Thornton, for it does not agree with me. I get drunk on a drop of the stuff.'

'Perhaps you would rather some tea?'

'No, for I shall only stay a few moments.'

Lytton was quite charmed by her forthright honesty. Her hair was snow white and the plain navy gown she wore sat well upon her. She balanced on the very edge of the leather wingchair nearest the fire. Her knuckles were white as she screwed her hands together, fingers full of substantial rings.

'My grandson will return to Highwick within the week to lick his wounds, I suspect. His father was a bully and he is turning out just the same. Don't have offspring, Thornton. They can only be a disappointment.'

'You have other children?'

'No. My only daughter was killed years ago with her family while journeying in Europe.' She did not continue and there was a shake in her voice that had not been there before.

'But enough of all that. I have come with a gift for you. A swap if you like for the stallion you sent back to me. This one is a mare. I have named her Countess, a personal vanity, I suppose, but I find it difficult to imagine her being called anything else.'

'I did not expect repayment.'

'No one has ever done such a kindness for me before. More normally I am out of sorts with the world, but you have restored my hope. I will tell my grandson that if there are any more outbursts like the one you encountered I shall cut him off entirely from the largesse of my own personal fortune. He was a difficult sullen boy who has turned into the same sort of man. My son's son. Two peas in a pod.'

She stood at that and collected herself. 'Before I go, though, I should like to ask you one question. You have been seen in the company of an unusual healer, a Miss Annabelle Smith by all accounts. I am presuming she was the woman I briefly encountered the other day as you walked to your carriage and I should very much like to meet with her.'

'I am afraid she is rather reclusive, my lady.'

'It is said she resides in one of your apartments?'

'She did, but she left with her aunt and gave no forwarding address.'

'Could you give her a message from me?'

Bringing out a sealed envelope from her reticule, she handed it over. 'It is a private correspondence, Thornton, so if time passes and you truly do not see her then I trust you will burn it. But I sincerely hope she may be contacted in some way.'

The day just got stranger. Did the Countess wish for some medical advice? he wondered. She looked quite hale and healthy, the tone of her skin radiant and her eyes clear.

Everything that concerned Annabelle Smith always had that edge of mystery and here it was again.

'I shall do my best.'

When she stood Lytton saw desperation in her eyes, an emotion so strong that he almost stopped her to ask what is was she wanted from Annabelle. But manners prevented such a direct and inappropriate enquiry.

A few moments later when her carriage pulled away from Portman Square the bright livery caught his eyes, gold against blue. Had not Roberts mentioned something of the same colours on the conveyance that had knocked Annabelle down on the Whitechapel Road?

Coincidence was often not the quirk of fate it purported to be. He had learnt that fact over his life many a time. Summoning his valet, he asked him to find Harold Roberts, the kitchen hand serving at the Stephens's residence, and bring him to the town house.

Energy suddenly filled him and he felt a shift in his world as he walked back inside, the small thin missive in his hand with its red wax seal, monogrammed and beribboned. Taking a book from his library which depicted the seals and crests of all the great families of the *ton*, he finally found the Huntington seal.

Apart from the colours there had been some talk at the scene of the shape of a ship on the top of the crest. This family crest contained all the elements spoken of. Fury began to fill him and this was followed by pure and utter worry. If Huntington was behind all this, Lytton knew he would not stop trying to hurt Annabelle.

But why would he? Tennant-Smythe's connections to his sister had thrown him off track, but he suddenly saw that the truth in the Earl's attempts on Annabelle's life lay in another direction entirely.

She had told him she felt someone had been following her and Shay had once mentioned seeing Huntington watching her in Regent Street. The Dowager Countess's visit and letter was another clue in the correlation of a link between Annabelle and the family as was her own admission of travelling in France and of her parents never returning home. They died there, she had told him, and he had known she was not telling him everything.

Annalena Tennant-Smythe had said her daughter had been killed along with her family while journeying in Europe and there had been more than a shake in her voice, too, hidden things as apparent as what she admitted.

A granddaughter. A blue-eyed dimpled

granddaughter in much the same mould as she herself must once have been.

Swearing he stood, helping himself to a brandy and downing the lot. Did Annabelle know any of this?

Other clues began to fall through the air. The family name was Tennant-Smythe and hers was Smith.

My God, if she was the lost heiress, then Huntington might have a great deal of motivation to see her gone, especially given his grandmother's lack of knowledge of her being here in England. How had he found out? How could have he known?

From seeing her at Portman Square probably while attempting to get in to see his sister, for Larkin had spoken of a gentleman who failed to leave a card but who had come calling twice.

That particular realisation had him thumping his glass down hard on the table. It was his fault Annabelle had been recognised. If he had never asked her to call on his sister, she might have simply stayed hidden in the streets of Whitechapel, just one of the thousands of poor who plied the area with their trade.

Yet she deserved a place, a family, an awareness of who she was and how she had disappeared. She needed to be given the choice as to where she would turn next, options in a life that was at present becoming more and more difficult.

But first he needed to find her. Money brought opportunity and he had a lot of it. He also had a reason now to make her listen and to tell her the truth of her past. It was not just for his sake now, this need to see her again, but for her own. He would begin with Mrs Rosemary Greene and then work his way through all of Annabelle's acquaintances that he knew of.

He was glad when Larkin announced that Roberts was waiting outside. Here was another source of information, another way of swaying this matter in his favour.

When the lad was shown in Lytton asked him to sit. He did so with a look of concern on his face.

'Don't be alarmed, Roberts. You are here because I need to find Annabelle Smith and quickly. She is in danger and she does not know of it.'

'Like the carriage accident and the fire, my lord. I said to my mother it did not look like coincidence to be hit twice like that and so quickly.'

'Precisely. I think I know the man who is behind these attacks and I need to keep her safe.'

Harold Roberts nodded. 'She has left London for Oxford, my lord, and is currently residing in the house of my mother's sister with her aunt. I will write you out the address.'

'I won't forget this, Roberts, and I promise I shall do everything in my power to make sure that she is not harmed.'

'I know you will, your lordship. She needs a friend.'

An hour later Lytton was in Hyde Park near the Serpentine. He knew Lady Catherine Dromorne would be walking here as she did each Tuesday at about three o'clock in the afternoon and he needed to see her before he departed for Oxford.

Spotting her standing over by the lake, he was relieved when she asked her accompanying maid to drop back and allow them some sense of private conversation.

'I have been thinking of what you said, Thorn, about us being friends. Perhaps on my side there has been the want for more, but on yours—'

He butted in. He had neither the time nor the inclination to make this any other than it was. 'For me you were always just a friend, Catherine. A woman whom I enjoyed talking with.'

'The thing is that now I find myself thinking that perhaps I should want more than only friendship.'

God, Lytton thought, was she saying what he hoped she might be? Was she realising the lack in their relationship would never sustain them over years of union?

'So I wondered if perhaps we might meet quietly somewhere, perhaps at your house, and we could...do more than kiss.'

The shock of her suggestion coming hard on the heels of an easy road to freedom hit him.

'Perhaps if we took our relationship to the next level we might discover important things, things we would both be thrilled with. I do not wish to lose you, Thorn, but I have heard rumours...'

She stopped, colouring a little and turning her gaze away.

'Rumours?'

'That the Whitechapel healer has taken your fancy and you have installed her as your new mistress in your apartments in Kensington.'

'I haven't. That is an untruth.'

'She is apparently very beautiful and clever. You were seen fighting for her honour on the streets not long ago. It seems that Lord Huntington came off much the worse for your intervention?'

He could say nothing of Lucy and her relationship with Tennant-Smythe and so he had to allow Catherine to believe that it was for Annabelle's sake that he had gone into battle.

'It got me thinking, you see. I would not wish for a milksop husband who could not protect me. I found your behaviour quite arousing, Thorn, arousing enough to want to have this conversation with you.'

God. He did not quite know how to go on from here.

Nothing was progressing as it should. His intentions. His future. His hope for a simple way out of a relationship that was becoming increasingly fraught.

He wanted Annabelle. He wanted to sit and talk with her and take her in his arms and kiss her. He wanted her blue eyes and her dimples and her softness and the way she managed people, with care and with kindness.

'I admire Miss Smith greatly.'

'I imagine that most people do. She is, after all, skilled at the arts of healing and is a herbalist of some note.' A coldness crept into her voice and Lytton brought the matter to hand.

'Whatever it takes for you to release me from my promise of a marriage I will do it. I do not love you like that, Catherine, and I never will. One day you might be thankful for my honesty.'

'But not this day, Thornton. I think you have played me as a fool.'

'It was not my intention to do that and I am sorry.'

'I am, too. Mama has advised me that I should

hang on to you no matter what. She does not think I shall ever receive a better offer.'

'What do you think?'

'I do not know any more. There is no handsome rich suitor waiting for me to turn you down and my options are dwindling.'

My God, he suddenly thought. *This is what I would be stuck with for ever were I to marry Catherine. Compromise and disappointment.* And just like that he could no longer do it, no longer pretend anything.

'I will not marry you, Catherine, on any grounds at all and we need to find a way forward that allows us both some dignity.'

'My father will be furious.'

'But it is not his life he is ruining. It is ours. What would you want to do most in the world if anything were possible?'

'Travel. Get away from my parents. I would like to go to Europe like your sister, see the sights, learn about the world.'

'I would pay for you to do that if you would break off the betrothal. I could make it possible for you to join Prudence and her husband in Italy.'

'How much would you pay?'

He should be frowning at her about-turn, but he wasn't. Instead he understood just how narrow was his miss with disaster and how close he had come to allowing responsibilities to dictate his happiness.

His mother and father had hated each other and so had his grandparents. Every single generation of Thorntons that he could remember were tarred with the same brush of disappointment and this was the tragedy in his blood, the true curse of the Earldom.

'Send me a receipt, Catherine.'

'My withdrawal from being linked to your name will be on the grounds that I no longer found you suitable. Perhaps you began to bore me and I felt a lifetime in your company would be unsustainable.'

'I'd agree to anything.'

'I will say you were simply not the man I hoped you to be and that I made a lucky escape.'

'I should not refute it.'

Lytton in truth did not care what she said as long as it allowed him his freedom.

'Then this is goodbye.' Tears were sliding down her cheeks.

He nodded and left her in the park in the sunshine before sending messages to both Aurelian and Shay.

They came quickly and were both curious.

'I am no longer promised in any way to Lady Catherine Dromorne and the relief is so great I have been walking on air. She will go travelling and no doubt slander my name across the *ton*, but I do not care. All I can see is freedom.'

'We didn't think you would go through with it, Thorn, for your heart was so plainly not in it.' Shay's words were quietly said.

'And that is what brings me to the reason for this meeting. I think Huntington was the one who was trying to get rid of Miss Smith. His grandmother, the Dowager Countess, came to see me yesterday and there were things she said that got me thinking.'

'And the point of all this?' Shay looked puzzled.

'I think he is dangerous to Annabelle. He has

tried to kill her twice and something tells me he will try again.'

'Why?'

'Annabelle Smith is somehow entwined with the Tennant-Smythe family. After doing some research I discovered that the Dowager Countess's daughter was lost with her husband in a carriage accident on the coast in the south of France. The thing is there was a young daughter travelling with them and she was never heard of again.'

Aurelian helped himself to a drink. 'But you think you may know what happened to her, Thorn?'

'At a guess I would say it is Annabelle Smith, but she has gone to ground. Before she disappeared I intimated that I wanted to marry her, Shay, and she refused.'

A whoop of delight was not what he expected.

'Finally. Right from the first moment of seeing her Celeste and I knew she was the one for you. So where is she now?'

'In Oxford. I got her address today and am leaving London in two hours.'

'To bring her back here?'

'No. To reunite her with her grandmother. I sent the Dowager Countess a message just before you came.'

'And Huntington?'

'Is in London with a broken nose and arm. For this moment he will be going nowhere.'

'Giving you a clean slate to fashion a reunion?'

'And to make sure that Annabelle has her rightful place again. The grandmother is a fierce woman. I doubt when Annalena Tennant-Smythe knows the whole story of his attempts on her granddaughter's life that a broken nose and arm are all the Earl will be left with. I have sent her a letter telling her of my plans to see Annabelle and I hope she might join me on the journey north.'

Two hours later he drove north with all haste, the horses his finest and the promise of more on the road to Oxford. The Dowager Countess sat beside him and in his hand was the bracelet of turquoise that he had given to Annabelle a week before.

* * *

Belle sat down against the south side of the wall beyond the garden to find some shade and leaned against it.

Here for a moment she was alone and unwatched. Here the sadness that had accompanied her since leaving London could be allowed some release as the thickness of sorrow choked away breath and pretence.

He was lost to her now, the Earl of Thornton, gone perhaps to marry a woman he had been long promised to. The tears came quietly, rolling down her cheeks in a stream of bewilderment. One finger covered her lips and she felt him there, real and warm, his breath against hers and his golden eyes watching closely.

It seemed as if the air she took no longer was enough and that she might die of the sadness and of her empty unending future. Her hand closed across her mouth to stop sound. This is what aloneness felt like. She huddled around its pain until there was no feeling left and the spent emotions had run their course.

Then she stood and wiped her eyes and her face on the material of her skirt, replacing agony with a tight smile. The world would see only this. She had been abandoned once and she could weather it twice, she swore it under the grey summer skies.

She returned half an hour later to the house of Mrs Roberts's sister where two rooms had been set aside for herself and her aunt. Mary Humphries was kind and hospitable, and although the dwelling was small it was scrupulously clean and very central to the town.

They could stay here for a little while or at least until the cough her aunt had been afflicted with had lessened. Then they would travel further north. Away from London and from Lytton Staines, the Earl of Thornton. Away from the possibility of her ever seeing him again.

The knock on the door came at around six o'clock just as they were sitting down for some soup and bread.

'I am not expecting anyone at all,' Mary said as she got up to answer it. 'Though sometimes Mr Browne from up the street pops in for a quick conversation. He has been lonely since his wife died so perhaps I could ask him in to join us.'

Annabelle smiled and thought again what a good person Mary Humphries was. Alicia simply frowned and resumed drinking her soup. Her aunt had closed in on herself after the fire in Whitechapel and had not welcomed human discourse of any sort ever since. Another worry. Her world was falling to pieces and she had no way of stopping it.

Lytton's voice at the doorway made Belle stand, shock running across her body in small tremors, her heart almost jumping from her chest. In a house this size he looked huge and important and vital. The travelling clothes he wore underlined his intent and when he removed his hat his hair fell in all the shades of gold and brown across the whiteness of his collar and an artfully arranged neckcloth.

'Ladies.' A lord of manners and charm. 'I am very pleased to find you here.' He looked directly at her.

She could not speak, any reply frozen in her throat. The last time they had met he had discussed marriage. Today he was all business and formality. Her hand gripped the back of the chair so that she would not fall.

'I wonder, Mrs Humphries, if you allow me a few minutes alone with Miss Smith and her aunt? My carriage is available outside to take you to any eating establishment in Oxford that you might name and partake in a meal with the compliments of myself, the Earl of Thornton?'

'Of c-course, your lordship.' Mary Humphries was flustered, allowing the Thornton manservant to lead her out of her own dining room and closing the door snugly behind them.

Then there was only silence and disbelief and that same longing that had been present in every single meeting between them so far.

Swatting it away, she took a step towards him.

'Why are you here, my lord? What could you possibly want with us here in Oxford?'

Alicia stood beside her, jarred out of mental ennui. It was like those hour glasses with the sand sifting through time, one second empty and the next completely full, turned into the new position, brought back in to life.

'She will not marry you, Lord Thornton. She cannot.'

'Tante.' God, this was going far worse than even she could have imagined it, Thornton's glance hardening at her aunt's words, the line of his mouth tighter.

'I have brought a visitor with me, Annabelle. I think she is someone who you need to meet.'

An old woman then came in to the room before she could say yes or no, helped in by one of Thornton's servants.

'This is the Dowager Countess of Huntington, Annalena Tennant-Smythe.'

Annalena? The name in her mother's Bible?

The newcomer was beautiful, her eyes blue and clear. Her hair was silver white and tied beneath a small hat into a chignon, the strands catching the light so that they glinted.

'Hello, my dear. You may not recognise me, but I think… I think I would always know you.' Tears had pooled in her eyes and her voice shook. 'When you were little you used to call me Nannalena.'

Nannalena? The echoes of the name were

there from long ago and Belle strained for more of the memory.

Come back to me, little one, come back when you can.

This was the woman who had said that to her, all that time before. The hands, the rings with the sapphires upon them, the eyes that were the same as her own. She breathed in. Even the smell was the same. Lost. To her. A lifetime ago.

The room began to swirl around, upending balance and sense. Belle tried to find a place to cling to and then the Earl's arms were around her, lifting her up, his jacket beneath her cheek, binding her to him. The sofa came under her and a blanket was found, warm and thick to take away her shakes. Her fingers threaded into Thorn's and she held on for all she was worth, the only centre in her out-of-control world.

'Don't go. Please.' She whispered the words and he smiled.

'I won't.'

The older woman sat now in a chair next to the sofa. 'I am sorry to give you a fright, Anna, but I have had rather a big one myself.' A handkerchief was in her grasp now and she dabbed at her eyes.

Anna? Her name? Anna Buchanan. She remembered that, too. Lady Anna Elizabeth Tennant-Buchanan.

'Who are you?' Her voice was working again, but even as she asked the question she understood exactly who this was.

'I am your grandmother. Your mother Elizabeth was my daughter and I have never been able to find you though I have searched and searched.'

'Where?'

Thorn balanced on the arm of the sofa and she looked up at him as though she needed confirmation on all that was being said. He nodded, allowing her belief.

'In Europe. Your parents died in a carriage accident near Marseilles in France twenty-seven years ago and there was never any sign of you, but I always prayed and hoped. And now...well... Thornton has brought you home to me and I cannot thank him enough.'

'How did you know?' This query was for the Earl.

'Your cousin was responsible for both the carriage accident and the fire. He wanted you gone, I suspect, before his grandmother got word of you. It seems that to divide even a little of your grandmother's wealth was untenable to him.'

The Dowager Countess frowned and was about to speak when Aunt Alicia moved forward to stand in front of her.

'Anna was delivered to me by a nun from the Notre-Dame de la Nativité in the village of Moret-sur-Loing. She said your daughter had brought the child in to be safe from her violent husband, for they had both been hurt by his fury.'

'I warned her. I warned Elizabeth so many times, but she would not listen.' Annalena Tennant-Smythe's voice was shaky and Annabelle reached out at the pain she could hear, her fingers cupping the small fragile hand. Her skin felt like crinkled paper but warm.

'Your father was a handsome man and my daughter was head over heels in love before he'd said his first words. I had my reservations about such a whirlwind romance, but he was charming and well born and so...' She tailed off. 'George Buchanan hit her once at Highwick, but Elizabeth would not hear a word against him. He was a Scottish earl and the family held extensive lands in the hills to the north of Edinburgh and after they left with you late one night I never saw them again. My husband was a violent man, too, so perhaps she was drawn to someone of a similar character to her father. I never forgave myself for the loss of a daughter and a granddaughter and then to have you back, alive after all these years...' She could not carry on.

Annabelle took a breath and began to explain. 'My mother saved me, I am sure of it, for when she delivered me to the small village outside of Paris she made the nuns promise that they would look after me until she could come back. Tante Alicia has done her very best to keep me safe ever since.'

'Then I have you to thank, too, Alicia. There are no words to say what I feel, but...'

Reaching out, Annalena hugged her aunt. Alicia's own arms came around the Countess's back and they clung on to each other, two older women caught in the storm of family disappointment, violence, greed and love.

'I did listen out for strangers who might have come to Moret-sur-Loing to find Annabelle, but they never arrived. I only wanted the very best for her.' Her aunt sounded exhausted, but she also sounded relieved.

The circle of life and lies had come fully around. She was no longer Annabelle Smith but Anna Elizabeth Tennant-Buchanan, the granddaughter of a countess, this old woman whose quiet bravery was astonishing.

Thorn was a huge part of it, too, for without him this would not be happening. It was his cleverness that had placed all the pieces of the puzzle together after making the connections.

She was a lady now, a woman of the *ton* with titles from the peerage on both sides of her family; all the reasons she had rejected the idea of being married to the Earl of Thornton in the first place. Yet there was a sadness in his eyes as she felt him unlink her fingers and stand back.

'I shall leave you in the hands of your family, Annabelle. Your grandmother can protect you now. Alicia will travel with you also back to the Huntington seat in Essex and this is how it should be.'

'You won't come with us?' Terror struck her.

'No, but I shall be there in London when you are introduced to society. Shayborne and Celeste shall stand with you as will Aurelian and Violet and you will be a sensation. No one will equal you and this is your birthright.'

He said the words in the way that made it certain he wanted no argument. He stated it as a goodbye, too.

Her grandmother was nodding, as was her aunt, the two of them a formidable pair.

Had her new circumstances made him waver, the reality of being aligned with a woman who was the cousin of the man who had mistreated his sister too onerous to contemplate?

She felt marooned by Thorn's indifference and by his willingness to leave, to simply walk out and desert her here while he returned to London.

She could understand none of it and the initial warmth of finding family began to fade under the realisation that she was losing the only man she would ever love.

He had never said he loved her, however, and he did not now. She went to stand, but her grandmother held her back.

'I asked Thornton for some time, Anna, and he promised it.'

Chapter Thirteen

Once back in London Lytton went straight to
the town house of the Huntingtons in Grosvenor Square and demanded to see Albert
Tennant-Smythe.

'He is indisposed, my lord. The doctor has
just left.'

'Tell the Earl it would be worth his while to
get up. Tell him I will wait ten minutes.' He
handed across his card.

'Yes, your lordship.'

His name was noted and uncertainty flared,
but the servant strode up the stairs to relate the
message none the less as Lytton waited.

Four minutes later Tennant-Smythe was before him, sporting two black eyes, an arm in a
thick bandage and a broken nose.

'If you are here to finish the job on me,

Thornton, then you'd best be getting on with it. As you can see I am in no condition to resist and—'

Lytton interrupted him. 'I am not going to gaol because of the sorry likes of you, Huntington. Your attacks on Annabelle Smith are repugnant and vile. While I would love to wrap my hands around your neck and squeeze the life from you, I also realise the sheer stupidity of such an action. I want you gone. From England. For ever. I have first-hand accounts of your part in the carriage accident in Whitechapel and I believe that it was you who set the fire in White Street. I have enough evidence to have you flung into gaol for a good many years, yet to drag you through the mire of your misdeeds would impinge upon your grandmother and cousin who are innocents in the face of all the crimes you have committed.'

The other swallowed at that and real fear crossed in to his eyes.

'Your cousin has been reunited with her grandmother and they have retired to Highwick together. Annalena Tennant-Smythe knows in intimate detail all that has taken place and to say she is ill pleased is putting it mildly. However much I would like to see you rot in gaol personally, I am of the opinion that complete ruin often promotes a misguided and unwelcome notion of revenge and so I am here to offer you an alternative. Leave England within the next few days accompanied by two servants of your choice and I shall provide you with enough money to start again. In America, perhaps. Or somewhere else as equally far-flung. Your choice.'

'Why would you do that?' His sneer did not look nearly as pronounced now.

'I told you. I want you gone. I do not want the Huntington family to be caught up in a scandal just as much as I wish my own not to be. If you do return, everything I hold on the choices you have made shall be offered to the magistrate here in London, immediately, and I shall be baying for your blood.'

He looked at his watch. 'You have ten seconds to decide your next course of action, Huntington. Starting now.'

In three seconds his answer came.

'I accept.'

'My man shall visit you tomorrow with a substantial bank draft. He shall want the name of the ship you have decided to take and the destination you will travel to before he hands it over to you.'

'I am sorry...'

'I do not want your apologies, Huntington, I just want you gone.'

In his carriage a few moments later Lytton leant back against the leather and looked out across the London streets. Part of him shook with the need to simply plunge a sharp knife through the chest of the Earl, but the other more sane part warned against it.

He must do everything he could now to safeguard Annabelle's name. She did not need scandal or foolishness or shame. Gossip would be rife about her past and her unexpected return to London society and he wanted her to have a place here, a home and a family.

He had promised the Dowager Countess on the way to Oxford that he would allow her to show her granddaughter her birthright before seeing her again. An introduction into a society ready to pick a stranger to pieces, no matter how illustrious their family, needed to be handled carefully and with exactly the right set of circumstances and he did not want his relationship with Lady Catherine Dromorne to be part of the equation. Setting Annabelle up in his old apartment had been a mistake, too, he knew that now and by withdrawing from her life completely until she came out any rumours might be allayed.

But he felt alone and desolate and his interview with Huntington had left him edgy and furious.

When Annabelle had taken his hand he had wanted to simply pick her up and take her home, for after days of not seeing her he was anxious to know that she was safe and well. The shock of her grandmother's reappearance had taken its toll on her, too, he could see that it had, but he could also decipher a sense of excitement and belonging that had not been there before.

With the Earl gone Lytton had made sure that she would stay safe and for now that was all he could do. He needed to let Annabelle go in order to find her again and allow her time to know who she truly was.

Would she still choose him? This query wound around in his head like a curse, for he knew that she would be fêted and admired by every unmarried red-blooded man of the *ton*.

But a promise was a promise and he meant to keep his word. In six weeks the Dowager Countess Annalena Tennant-Smythe would bring out her granddaughter at a splendid ball in the family town house in Grosvenor Square and he would then make it clear to her exactly how he felt.

Chapter Fourteen

The European silk gown she wore had been primped and fussed with for hours, so that the floating sleeves sat just right and the organza top skirt embellished with embroidered leaves fell in a draped and classic fashion. Peach suited her, she decided, the soft shade picking up the darkness of her hair and the whiteness of her skin. Ribbons of the same shade were threaded through the high waist and the neckline sat off her shoulders, plunging in both the back and the front.

Annabelle tried to pull it up a little so that it did not seem quite so low, but the dressmaker was having none of it, instantly taking it back to where it had been and admonishing her gently.

'With skin like yours, my lady, and a bosom worth looking at, there should be no reason why one would not show it off. So often I dress girls with far less charm and a lot more un-called-for arrogance. You will be the belle of the ball and your grandmother will be thrilled, for even in Paris at this moment I doubt one would find a more beautiful gown or a more beautiful woman to fill it.'

Belle thought she would have to take the word of Madame Hervé, for she had no true idea at all of the latest trends in ball gowns and neither did she have much interest in finding out. But the whole idea of being such a centre of attention filled her with anxiety.

She just wanted this first foray into society over so that life as she had known it might return even in a small measure. She could not believe the time it had taken across the past weeks to learn the steps of the dances undertaken at the great balls or the complex eating habits and the rules and manners associated with being a lady that were so ludicrously numerous and unfailingly exact.

Would Thorn be here tonight? Would he ask her to dance? Would he like the new and improved Lady Anna Elizabeth Tennant-

Buchanan? There was not much left of the woman he had known in Whitechapel.

He had not come to Highwick. He had not arrived at the doorstep of the Hall to see her. It was only this week that her grandmother had explained she had asked the Earl of Thornton for a promise not to visit so that the life she had lost all those years ago might be able to be fully realised again. Had he let her go? Had he moved on? He had not mentioned love when he had tossed out his words on marriage in the house of his inventor friend and the fact that he had installed her in the rooms of his former mistress didn't bear great witness to any higher order of intention.

He had wanted her, she knew that, and wanted her badly. Badly enough to even propose his idea of a union?

Her grandmother had come into her room now and she had a long burgundy case in her hands.

'These were my mother's, Anna, and her mother's before her. Would you wear them tonight?'

She flicked open the catch and the necklace

and matching earrings of sapphires and diamonds inside were astonishing. Belle had never owned any jewellery apart from the bracelet that she had returned to Thorn.

'They are beautiful.'

'They will show the world that you are sponsored by me and in the *ton* that is not a small thing.'

The last six weeks had been eye opening. Her grandmother was a woman of culture and pride and passion. But as well as all those things she had taken her and her aunt beneath her wings and made sure that they had wanted for nothing.

Alicia had flourished, the chesty cough that had plagued her in Whitechapel for years and years had all but disappeared in Highwick. It was one of the reasons her aunt had not journeyed down to London to see her out in society. She simply could not bear the thought of the London air aggravating her lungs again, the purity of that in the countryside much more to her liking.

Annabelle could scarcely believe her change of circumstances. Now instead of sharing a small rented dwelling in Whitechapel, her grandmother had allotted each of them luxurious suites in Highwick Manor and dressed them both as befitted their station.

She had not seen the Earl of Huntington once and neither had her grandmother and for that they were both actually extremely grateful. She prayed to God that she would not come across him at the ball tonight, for he was one of the few people in the *ton* who would know that Miss Annabelle Smith and Lady Anna Buchanan were one of the same. Thorn's friends, of course, held that same knowledge, but she did not imagine them to be a threat at all.

She was nervous. Nervous of making a mistake. Nervous of not being all her grandmother hoped she could be. Nervous of seeing Thorn's indifference or even dislike.

'We will go downstairs in fifteen minutes, my dear,' Annalena said as she fastened the necklace and turned her to the mirror.

She looked so very different. She looked like a lady. She looked as if she was born to be in the peach-silk gown with her hair pulled up at the back and a series of ringlets curling around her face. Fastening the earrings with shaking hands, Belle turned to pick up her reticule. It held a handkerchief, lavender salts and a dance card and was embroidered with peach-coloured ribbons to match her dress.

Like the fairy tales in the books she had read in the Tennant-Smythe library of princesses and godmothers and cruel circumstances that had been altered for the better on a trick of magic.

Like Cinderella going to the ball.

She had heard the carriages drawing into Grosvenor Square across the past half an hour and knew the Countess had invited above two hundred guests to her grand and formal evening. The sound of conversation and music could be heard here upstairs, laughter punctuating the hum every now and again.

After this there would be no turning back.

A knock at the door brought the maid in with a calling card.

'The Honourable Percy Rawlings is in the room outside, my lady.'

'Oh, good, send him in. My brother has offered to be our escort tonight and he is always very good at these large occasions.'

Belle had met Percy a number of times already, the affable man a firm favourite of the household. She was glad they would have him to lead them down and said so as he appeared.

'Well my love,' he returned quickly, 'your rediscovery has been one of the nicest things to have happened in my life and I know you will be a huge success. It can seem daunting, but Annalena and I shall chase away any wolves.'

Her grandmother brought them each a chilled drink of lemonade and they clinked the crystal glasses together.

'To family,' her grandmother said, 'and to happiness. To Elizabeth, too, wherever she is for making certain in the only way she could that her daughter should return to Highwick.'

The poignant reminder of her mother made Belle smile gently. 'I wish Mama could have been here.'

'She is,' her grandmother returned. 'She is here in you.'

Lytton had come to the Tennant-Smythe ball with Aurelian, Violet, Shay and Celeste. He had come early and found a spot at the end of the room by some pillars. He had refused every drink offered for he needed to be at his best tonight with all his wits about him.

Violet next to him noticed his latest refusal and smiled. The hope he could see on Violet's face made him even more nervous and he wished like hell he had not taken Aurelian's advice and asked for help on the words Annabelle might most want to hear.

Violet had been kind, he would give her that, but her instruction to him to allow Annabelle to see all his fears and worry held a sort of hopeless impossibility here at a very public ball. Celeste had been just as confusing. Her counsel had consisted of using the sort of prose he'd never felt comfortable with and at the end of the conversation he even wondered if she might be jesting. He could not ask Aurelian or Shay to clarify things, either, for he was so far out of his depth with the raw emotions it was almost like drowning.

But he had taken his own steps to convince Annabelle to favour him, the deed in his pocket holding the sort of weightiness he knew she might well understand, though even that thought held its complications.

Pray to God she had not changed. The mantle of being a lady would be a heavy one and there would be so many possibilities now open to her. Had Miss Annabelle Smith from Whitechapel been supplanted entirely by this new version? He had not felt this nervy since he was a youth and he swallowed away the frantic beat of his heart.

The music began suddenly heralding the arrival of the guest of honour and all eyes looked upwards to a grand staircase at the end of the room upon which three figures were now descending.

Annabelle stood on the right, a shimmering beauty in a gown of a colour he had rarely seen before. Her hair was up, but the length of it hung around her face in curls before reaching down her back. She looked nothing like the woman he had known in London, dressed in her ill-fitting hand-me-downs and her unusual scarves. Yet though the outward trimmings might be different, there was still that calm centred sureness that had always attracted him and a good sense that was so very beguiling. Others felt it, too, and a hush covered the room.

When people moved in for introductions he saw that she was enjoying it, her hand raised in just the right way, words tripping from her lips to make them laugh and lean forward and listen. It was easy to see the conquests and the triumphs as those she spoke with kept returning to her side.

The victory of beauty and grace and something else far less definable.

Inclusion was the nearest he could come to the meaning of what he sought. She did not have airs and arrogance, but kindness and acumen.

Suddenly Lytton could no longer bear it and, excusing himself from his friends, he walked towards the French doors to one side of the room and out on to a wide balcony. His fingers grasped on to the stone balustrade. He felt nauseous and hot. If this went badly…?

Others had come out now for some respite from the packed and noisy salons and he could not help but hear what they were saying.

'Lady Anna is the most beautiful woman I have ever laid eyes on and she is also so very substantial. Her conversation is nothing like the inane exchanges we have forever been subjected to.'

'Thank God, I say. Did you see Frederick Alley? He was smitten by her and so was Aleric Carswell.'

'As was every other unmarried male of the *ton* and a good few of the married ones besides. Where the hell has she been hiding, do you think?'

'In France, according to the Dowager Countess's brother. Near Paris, by all accounts.'

'She will be married before the month is out, that much I will say. I can see every eligible male formulating their troths as we speak.'

Lytton walked further away so that he would not hear them. She had been in the cold for so many years he needed her to enjoy the heat, to know what a success she was and to revel in it. Annalena Tennant-Smythe had done a sterling job with her granddaughter; her hair, her gown and her demeanour could not be faulted. She was the embodiment of a woman whom both males and females could warm to, the whole package with nothing at all missing.

He should leave now and allow her the choice of love. He had, after all, placed down his hand and failed and he wanted her to be happy. He should simply walk out and return home. She knew where he lived, after all, but had never come. There had been no contact between them whatsoever.

Annabelle saw the Earl of Thornton's friends approach her and looked around for him, disappointment rising. She had not seen him anywhere and she had been looking. With a sigh she took Celeste Shayborne's offered hand and thanked her for coming.

'I should have guessed you were a lost heiress, Lady Anna, the moment I met you. There were so many clues, after all.'

'Call me Anna and I am so pleased to see you all here.'

'Thorn didn't come up with us.'

'Oh, he is away from London, then?' Belle tried to keep the regret out of her words, but knew she had failed as Celeste shook her head.

'No. I mean he is here somewhere in this enormous room, but we seem to have lost him.'

'He has gone for a drink. A fortifying one, I imagine.' Aurelian now took up the conversation and there was laughter in his words. 'Though I am sure he will seek you out when the masses have fallen back a little.'

'It is rather a crush, isn't it?' Annabelle replied, wishing she might simply roam about the room in search of the elusive Earl.

'The sign of a successful debut, I would say. Shay imagines you will have myriad marriage proposals on the table by the morrow and whoever you choose would be undeniably lucky.'

'I sincerely hope that does not happen.' The words fell out of her mouth even though she knew honesty was not a particularly valued commodity here in the heartland of the *ton*.

Celeste began to laugh. 'I remember feeling exactly the same as did Violet. Have you met Aurelian's wife yet, Annabelle?'

The name made her smile and she turned to the newcomer, a beautiful woman with the reddest hair she had ever seen.

'No, I have not had the pleasure.'

'Oh, it is all mine, Lady Anna. I am so glad that your family found you and brought you home.'

No one else had quite said it like that all night and Annabelle instantly felt a connection with Violet de la Tomber. In the eyes of both these women she saw a vein of humour and irreverence, and a sort of half-hearted acceptance of the ways and oddities of the *ton*.

She wished she might have friends like them, friends who were honest and forthright and not at all bound by convention. She wanted to hold their hands and keep them both with her, human shields against the arrogance and snobbery that was so prevalent here.

'I hope Thorn will find me,' she suddenly said. It was far to familiar, she knew it was, and much too honest, but the hours were running down to midnight and she imagined that he might leave without even seeing her.

'He will.' Celeste spoke firmly. 'He is a good man who thinks you need the chance to shine in your own light without being shaded by his. But he will come when he understands the truth of what he feels, I know it.'

Her grandmother had joined the group now and asked if Annabelle would come to meet some old friends of hers. With nothing else to do but acquiesce, Annabelle followed her.

The clock had struck two before Thorn approached her. She was standing with Violet over to one side of the room and looked even more beautiful close up than she had at a distance.

When Violet saw him she quickly excused herself, giving him the chance of a moment of aloneness with Annabelle.

'You look beautiful.' Ridiculous words, but true.

'Thank you.' There was a half-smile on her lips.

'Would you like to dance?'

A waltz was just warming up and people all around them were taking to the floor. Dancing would give him some distraction and promised a few moments of uninterrupted closeness.

'I am still not particularly proficient at the steps so I hope you will not mind if I tread upon your feet.'

'I won't.'

He took the hand that she held out and she walked beside him. There were sapphires and diamonds around her neck and on her ears, the largesse of the Huntington family on display.

All the words he had practised to say fell away and he was left with silence, the music all around them, the lights above and the warmth of her body so close against his own.

They could have been dancing alone in a glade set in a far-off enchanted forest, bare of people. For a second he closed his eyes and just felt the shape of her fingers under the long white gloves as he breathed in a pervading scent of lavender. Opening them again, he saw that her hair shone dark beneath the lamps, the colour of wood under water or winter leaves underfoot.

Annabelle was matchless and original and completely herself. Her dimples showed up as deep shadows on each cheek.

'I thought you might not come, my lord. I imagined the night ending and still not seeing you...'

'I'm sorry. You were busy.'

'Not so busy that I could not thank the one man who has rescued me again and again, without recompense or reward.'

'It's been a lot quieter on that front lately.' The start of a smile surprised him, but then Annabelle had always had the ability to make him laugh. 'McFaddyen sends you his greetings.'

Her step was out of beat and they stumbled slightly, the movement bringing their bodies closer. He could feel the shape of her breasts under thin silk and drew in a breath. She had filled out and he had thinned down. There seemed to be no end to the comparison of differences.

'I brought you a gift.' He unlinked one hand and dug an envelope out from his pocket. 'Perhaps you might open it later?'

'Thank you.' The frown across her forehead made him want to lift his fingers and rub it away. He was pleased when she deposited the deed in her reticule, the peach ribbons adorning it twinkling in the light.

He wished that this dance might continue all night, the feel of her in his arms, the warmth of the summer evening, the way she allowed him to lead her around the room. The sheer closeness.

'You are a far better dancer than I am, my lord.'

'I've had years of practice.'

'I heard that Lady Catherine Dromorne has broken off your engagement. It seems she discovered you were not the man she thought you to be.'

'A fortunate detection. I think she is in Italy now with my sister Prudence, who has decided to stay on with her husband. I hope Catherine finds what she is looking for there.'

'Which is what?'

'Love. A soulmate. Someone to make life bearable. Someone to love her back.' He tried to keep the words light, but could not, and his fingers closed tighter around her own.

'You did not come and see me at Highwick? Not once?'

'Your grandmother asked it of me. She wanted a new start for you and all the possibilities that such a thing might entail.'

'Possibilities?'

'Choices, I should imagine, and options. A

selection of husbands to settle down with, a man who might suit your station and your inclination. It seems there are many here tonight who would like to show their hand.'

'I have already had one offer.'

His heart sank.

'Which I've decided to accept.'

God, he had lost her then and there was no way he could save what had been between them.

'Then I give you my congratulations, Lady Anna. I hope he deserves you.'

'Oh, I think he does.' Her voice held amusement.

'And I hope he knows how to make you happy.'

'That, too.'

She was smiling, which did not quite seem right. Annabelle had never been unkind before.

'He understands me, you see, as no other ever has and he protects me to the very core of his being. I could not imagine my life with anyone else. He is my perfect match and I think he knows that I am his as well.'

The small clues clicked into place and pleasure made his blood run hot.

'Annabelle?'

'Yes, Thorn.'

'Will you marry me as soon as I can procure a licence?'

She moved in closer. 'Why do you ask me?'

'Because I love you. Because there will never be anyone else for me. Because we belong together and without you I am only half a person.'

The music had stopped now but they stood there still, oblivious of what was happening around them, of the stares and the conjectures, of the growing puzzlement and the speculation.

'I love you, too, Thorn, and I have done since first Stanley tore your pink waistcoat in the front room at White Street.' She could see him swallow and take in breath and his hand shook beneath hers. 'I want children and a home with you and a family and for ever.'

'God.' The word sounded torn from the depths of hope.

'I think it's yes you are supposed to say and then you kiss me.'

He grabbed at her hand and, taking no care of the stares of all those around her, he pulled her from the room and into a small salon that sat on the other side of the doors they had just exited.

'Yes,' he said before his lips came down in ownership and tenure and Annabelle saw then all he had kept harnessed, the need and the want and even the fear.

The thin peach gown held no hope against his fervour as his hands clutched her to him, a grasp that gave the promise of never again letting her go.

Love.

Desperate. Shaking. Disbelieving. Unguarded.

She felt the tears on her cheeks even as he wiped them up with his finger.

'I will never leave you again, Annabelle. I thought...' He stopped. 'I thought after last time that you might not want to see me again.'

'Love me, Thorn.'

'I do. Desperately.'

This time she kissed him, bringing his head down and taking his mouth. The thrall that snaked through her was indescribable. He was hers and she was his and everything that came before now was as nothing. This day, this moment, this night was the beginning of the life she wanted, with a man whom she trusted and understood. An honourable man who would always protect her and always love her.

She took in breath as he pressed her against him, feeling the rustle of paper in her reticule.

'What is in your envelope?'

'Something I purchased for you. Something I think you will like.'

He let her go as she brought the paper from her bag. It was a deed for a property in Whitechapel, a place on the Whitechapel Road. Her name was the sole one written upon it.

'I thought you would suffer if you were unable to keep practising your particular kind of medicine and I wanted you to be independent and self-reliant even if it was not me you chose.'

She burst into tears and he looked surprised.

'You do not like it?'

'I love it. I love that you would think to do this for me, Thorn. It is simply perfect, the best wedding present I could ever imagine. But I want the deed changed. I want your name to be there, too, together.'

'Together,' he echoed and a new desperation assailed them. She could feel a growing hardness between his thighs and his breathing had changed.

'I want you.' This was said as a hoarse and raw troth, no question in it, though when the door unexpectedly opened they broke away from each other, their fingers still entwined.

'Anna?'

Her grandmother stood there with her greatuncle at her shoulder. Both looked more than surprised even as Thorn took charge of the situation and began to speak.

'I have asked your granddaughter for her hand in marriage and she has said yes. The ceremony will take place as soon as possible.'

Annalena came forward, an enormous smile on her face. 'I never imagined that this could be so wonderful, my dear. The Earl of Thornton as your husband is a perfect choice because he is kind as well as powerful and you will need that.'

Annabelle hugged her grandmother and then

she hugged Percy. There were tears in his eyes as he let her go.

'When will the wedding take place?'

'As soon as I can get a licence.' Thorn spoke, his voice filled with pride.

'I don't want it huge, Thorn. I want a small and intimate ceremony with just the family and a few friends and I would very much like it to take place at Highwick.'

Her grandmother looked delighted. 'Huntington has written to me from America and he said he will not return to England for a long while. I think it is for the best that he stays away. A recompense for the way he has behaved, perhaps?'

'A new beginning,' Thorn added as Rawlings shook his hand in congratulations.

'Shall we announce your intentions tonight with everyone present?' her grandmother asked.

'Yes.' Both she and Thorn said this at once.

Chapter Fifteen

Three weeks later

'You are the most beautiful bride that any man could hope for.'

Annabelle stood before him in her white-silk under-gown with flowers woven through her hair, the curls of which moulded around her waistline.

'When I am old and infirm and I cannot remember one other thing, I pray to God that I will remember this.'

They had been married three hours ago in the chapel at Highwick and had now retired to the suite in the east wing of the hall which had been reserved especially for them.

Aurelian had been his best man and Shay had been the groomsman. Annabelle had asked Lucy to attend her and Mrs Rosemary Greene had journeyed especially from Whitechapel to be her other bridesmaid. Lytton's brother David had come up from the school he'd recently returned to and had enjoyed the celebration, but Prudence his sister had not been able to make the trip from Italy under such short notice.

Belle held her marriage ring up to her new husband now, one finger turning the gold and sapphires so that they glinted in the light.

'I don't think that I could possibly be any happier.' Her voice was quiet and filled with a shyness that was new. 'But I need to tell you something before...' She stopped and blushed, an action so unlike her that he frowned.

'Tell me what?'

'I know I am ancient, but the thing is that I am still a virgin. I don't comprehend quite what you might want me to do though, as I've told you, I have read books and so I am not entirely unsullied...'

He brought his hand forward and ran a finger across her lower lip to stop the unending torrent of apprehension. She was nervous, for the skin on her arm had raised in to goosebumps.

'There is no right or wrong in making love, Annabelle. There is only truth.'

The air had changed around them now, from delight and joy to desire and need. Lytton could feel the blood thrum through his veins as he ran his finger down further across her chin and the long lines of her throat to rest on the rise of one breast covered in white silk.

The round firmness of it filled his palm and he flicked at her nipple, her head tilting back so that she closed her eyes, breathing with surprise and shock.

'It feels…hot.'

'And this?'

His hand pulled back the flimsy fabric and came in to the nakedness beneath. The hard bud of her grazed his skin and he took the firmness between one finger. 'Do you feel this?'

She only groaned in response.

'Or this?'

He had slipped the strap of her gown across her shoulders so that her breast was now visible and his mouth came around her, sucking gently.

Bright blue eyes flew open and her fingers came to rest upon his head.

'This is allowed?'

He laughed. 'This and so much more, my darling. Trust me.'

'I do.'

The sweetness of her answer tugged at him, her innocence and her purity. He had never once before made love to a virgin, for every woman he had bedded was well attuned in the ways of the joining of flesh.

This was different. Annabelle drove him wild even while he harnessed such a desperate need. She was soft and pliant and open and real. When his mouth fastened back on her lips he revelled in her.

His. The one word had his member standing firm against his thighs. He ached with the desire to possess her and he trembled with the necessity to take it slowly.

Drawing in breath, he pushed down the other strap so that the silken sheath fell in a pool to the ground. On her feet were silken slippers and in her hair were white gardenia buds, their scent beguiling and fragrant.

Fragrant like Annabelle with her dimples and her long dark hair, her swollen lips and the ivory of her skin whorled into redness by his mouth.

'Hell.' He couldn't keep his emotion in, the word surprising her.

Thorn was swearing again. Was there something wrong? Was there a flaw that she had never considered in her body, a defect that she had not understood before?

He looked heated and he was breathing quickly, his eyes darkened to a bruised brown and standing there before him, virtually unclothed while he was fully dressed, she suddenly felt...wicked.

Not wrong, no, not that, but revealing in a way that let him see right into her. Opening her legs, she tipped back her head, liking the feel of her hair heavy against the round of her bottom. A temptress. A siren. As far away from the careful and sensible Miss Annabelle Smith as she could have possibly come.

The sensuality of what was happening kept her still, her breath shallow even as all the parts inside her melted into feeling, sharp in one way and muted in another.

Take me, she wanted to say. Take me to the places I have only read about and let me know the magic between a man and a woman, between a husband and a wife.

The candles on the sideboard flickered, the scent of them heady. The grandfather clock in the corner struck the hour of six and a curtain billowed against the incoming breeze from an opened window letting in a slight but welcome breeze.

It slid across her body and Thorn laughed, his head coming down as he licked a trail where the zephyr had lingered, from navel to breast. The coldness left was almost painful and her breath banked. He would hurt her soon because all the books spoke of that. Ripped asunder and plundered. It was the way of men when they took. Her teeth began to chatter.

'Don't hurt me too much. Please.'

'Ah, sweetheart,' he replied and stood, unbuttoning the small garment that was left on her and peeling it away so that only nakedness remained, a single lacy garter at her thigh and a gold bracelet from her grandmother at her wrist.

With a soft, reassuring movement he opened her legs, her thighs spread against his hands, his fingers coming into the centre of her, a quiet intrusion, a small but determined assault. Then one was in her, up inside and joined with another. She felt the thickness of them and the stretching as they arched up deeper, his own body beginning to move against hers with the rhythm of his hand.

Not gentle now, but seeking. Her grasp came down to hold him there, her feelings growing wilder as he quickened. She could not breathe, could not move, could not escape from the plundering hardness, her heart thumping and the sweat building until there was nowhere left to go but up, up into trembling release, up into heaven and sweetness and relief. She could not stop her sounds, short guttural groans that made her breath swell and her stomach clench, hard inside, almost falling.

He simply picked her up then and took her to the bed, laying her down unresisting, the wetness on his fingers staining her skin with the musky smell of passion. Her own hand came to the place his had just been and the surprising wet made her gasp.

'It is your body welcoming mine, Annabelle. It is beautiful.'

He had taken off his shirt and his trousers followed, the fall unbuttoned and then gone. She had never seen a man before unclothed save in books, and flesh and blood was a lot more immediate than the marbled statues of ancient gods.

Scrambling up, she sat and he came in beside her, placing her hand upon him, so that she could feel the softness among the hard, familiarising her.

'It is just me, my love, ready for you. It might hurt a little at first, but then...' He stopped and she saw him swallow. 'But then we will fit. I promise it.'

Crossing his heart, he lifted her so that she sat astride him on his knee, a careful gentle lift. The tip of him rested in the place his fingers had been and then ventured deeper, stopping when the pain began.

'I love you.' His words were whispered against her cheek and he held her still, filling her, feeling her, helping her to understand the small and powerful questions of the flesh and waiting for a sign.

The throb of blood, the quickening beat of their hearts and this time when she moved he moved with her, in and out, deep and then deeper, the rush of lust, the answer to fear, the understanding of a reciprocal pleasure that bloomed deep between them.

Tipping her head, he looked straight into her eyes, their joining complete. 'Come with me, sweetheart. Come now.'

Another feeling rose. Not quiet. Not gentle. Not waiting. She rode him with her own need, pushing into fervour and intensity as waves of consummation crashed all around them, beaching on to the sands of love.

Complete. She felt as if her life had just begun in this second and as if every other moment before it had been leading to exactly this. She was spent and elated, she was exhausted and energised. She wanted to keep him inside her for all the hours of the night, beating in her, quenching the fire. There was no world around them save the one that was here and she never wanted to leave it.

'You are everything to me, Thorn.' The words were whispered as she kissed his neck. She wanted him again, violently. She wanted the feelings back, the power and the beauty.

He seemed to understand what it was she asked of him because he laid her down and then his mouth was there, his tongue, his breath, the softness of flesh and the urgency. Filled up with him her hand threaded through his hair and she moved, no rhythm now, but broken strokes and uneven.

When she climaxed this time she wondered if she might lose consciousness altogether as she stopped breathing and simply felt.

He was a magician and she was his assistant, a lover of such prowess that she could not grasp the consequence. When he sat up he kissed her mouth and she could taste herself on him.

'I feel like a king,' he finally said. 'The king of happiness.'

She laughed and stretched. 'The king of lovers, too.'

'A king with a queen who takes my breath away. Thank you, Annabelle, for everything.'

'Will it always be like this? Making love?'

'I hope so. Perhaps it is particular just to us, this elation, because I have never felt it before.'

'Then I am glad.'

She felt the shake of his humour. Joy in the marriage bed, complete and perfect.

'Others will know what is between us because it will be impossible to hide.'

'And when they guess they will be happy for us. We have both been lonely for so long. Besides, Aurelian and Shay both have women who complete them and perhaps we might help Edward find the same when he returns to England next year.'

'Your inventor friend?'

'You will like him. He has the same sort of enquiring mind as you have.'

'My aunt would say the same of you, Thorn.'

'Alicia seems a lot happier now and healthier, too.'

'She wants to run the clinic in Whitechapel. Rose is going to help her and Milly, our kitchen maid in White Street, will be a part of it, for she has not enjoyed her new job at the tannery. I also want to be involved as much as I can be.'

'I never doubted it.' His smile was kind.

'That's another reason why I married you. You believe in me and support me. I don't know what might have happened if I had never met you. I might have been sad for ever.'

'We would have met, Annabelle. I'd have made sure of it.'

Epilogue

One and a half years later

They sat by the fire on a cold January evening, the snow thick outside and the sky stormy. Aurelian, Violet, Shay, Celeste and all their children had left that very afternoon, having spent the Christmas holidays up at Balmain. Edward Tully was still here, though he was often out in the evenings.

'Where does Ed go at night?' she asked Thorn dreamily, sitting in his arms on the thick rug in their bedchamber and watching the flames.

'To drown his sorrows, I think, down at the village tavern. He is lonely and lonelier still in the company of all of us. I remember feeling exactly the same before I met you and for some time after. Happiness seems so elusive when you do not have it.'

A noise to one side of the room had her turning. 'Sleep is elusive, too, my darling,' she replied very softly so that Harry did not waken. At eight months their son was full of energy, but a very light sleeper. They had taken to having his cot in their room much against everyone's wishes, but for them it felt right.

Thorn's hand cupped around her stomach, easily accessed under the nightdress she was wearing.

'And this new little one? I wonder who this will be?'

'Ours,' she replied and leaned back to kiss him, surprised as always by the passion his small touches engendered. One and a half years together and the magic just kept on growing so that she felt the luckiest woman in all the world.

His family had come to Balmain this year and though she had always been close to Lucy, his mother, too, was beginning to thaw. Alicia had had her part in that, too, and Annalena as well, for the three of them had formed a close friendship and were often seen together talking.

A family.

All the pieces of it disparate, but forming a whole that was comforting and strong.

'Annalena had a letter from Huntington the other day.'

She felt him tense.

'He asks if perhaps he might visit us in the summer. He regrets all the things that he has done and wishes to make amends.'

'Is your grandmother happy with him coming?'

'She is. He has not been well and I think she worries for him.'

'And how do you feel, Annabelle?'

'He is my cousin. He should have a second chance.'

His arms folded around her, bringing her in closer, and she smiled. This was how life was supposed to be lived, with joy, hope and forgiveness. Passion, too, was a part of it and, turning, she slipped the nightgown from her shoulders and watched his eyes as the fire played over her breasts.

'My beautiful Countess,' he said as his mouth came upon her.

* * * * *

LET'S TALK

Romance

For exclusive extracts, competitions
and special offers, find us online:

 facebook.com/millsandboon

 @millsandboonuk

 @millsandboon

Or get in touch on 0844 844 1351*

For all the latest titles coming soon,
visit millsandboon.co.uk/nextmonth

Want even more
ROMANCE?

Join our bookclub today!

'Mills & Boon books, the perfect way to escape for an hour or so.'

Miss W. Dyer

'Excellent service, promptly delivered and very good subscription choices.'

Miss A. Pearson

'You get fantastic special offers and the chance to get books before they hit the shops'

Mrs V. Hall

Visit millsandbook.co.uk/Bookclub and save on brand new books.

MILLS & BOON